Bear in a Bakery

Liz Paffel

Contents

Bear in a Bakery

♥

One sexy carpenter bear shifter. One sassy human with a sweet, sweet cinnamon roll.

Allie Rowe is in a bind after drunk raccoons do a number on her business, Sticky Sweet Bakery. With a major event coming up, she can't afford to be out of commission... but she can't afford to fix things, either. Her meddling father thinks he'll play matchmaker when he hires sexy carpenter and bear shifter Dax Mitchell to lend a hand.

She's already played the rejected mate game, and isn't going there again, thanks. Bear shifters are trouble with muscles. Shifters are off limits!

Dax won't take no for an answer, making her wonder if he's helping from the kindness of his heart, or if he'll require some sort of repayment...

Dax is under pressure to take a mate before the fates rob him of his strength. His dying father's wish is to see his son mated. A staunch bachelor, Dax is inclined to change his mind when sexy, curvy Allie offers him a taste of her sweet roll.

When an unexpected enemy makes himself known, and time winds down on his chance to take a mate, Dax must decide how far he'll go to claim his fated mate.

Bear in a Bakery is a fun, fated mates paranormal romance featuring fated mates and lots of sticky sweet yumminess!

Chapter One

Bear shifters make terrible boyfriends.

Allie Rowe tossed her cell phone on the counter and put her head on her outstretched arms. She was two seconds from combusting over stress and leave it to her ex, Blake—the cockiest bear shifter in Colorado—to send her a passive-aggressive, *I understand you're busy again, but it makes me angry when you don't respond to my messages*, text. She was about to text back a picture of her sparkly, purple, rabbit-eared vibrator, lovingly named "The Rock" Johnson, with a comment that size did, indeed, matter.

Blake and his tiny cock could fuck off. She was over him. He'd rejected her after claiming she was his fated mate. Stupidly, she'd believed his bullshit until he tossed her aside like she was nothing.

She wouldn't put it past him to have something to do with the pair of drunk raccoons that turned her beloved Sticky Sweet Bakery into a rave two nights ago. She'd come in at four a.m. to start baking and found shredded curtains, claw marks in the wallpaper, the coffee bar destroyed, and condiment wrappers scattered everywhere. The furry assholes must have eaten the sugar packets and creamer tubs in a munchie frenzy. They'd chewed on trim and baseboards, gnawed holes in the wall, and dumped all three bistro tables onto their sides.

And that was just the customer area of the bakery. The kitchen hadn't fared much better with bowls and trays and cooking utensils dumped on the floor. Who knew raccoons under the influence could eat their way through a plastic bakery tub to consume five dozen chocolate chip cookies, and somehow manage to get into the ceiling tiles, pop them out of the frame, and leave gaping holes?

Her pretty pink and yellow store, with gingham curtains and original, hand-carved, white-washed wood trim, and original brick floor looked like someone had taken an axe to it. The damage was more than she could fix on her own. The décor and cosmetics, she could remedy. But the trim, ceiling, and damage to the walls would require a professional; one she couldn't afford. She'd already had a small electrical fire that jacked her business insurance rates. Add in this claim, and the premium would probably put her out of business.

Allie groaned. She was so screwed.

The bank notice she'd gotten today solidified that. The interest on her business loan was about to balloon well above what she was budgeted for. Ah, hell. It was all more to add to the Loser Allie List anyway. No matter how hard she tried, there was always another failure to add to the never-ending list of reasons why she couldn't get her life together. The scariest thing at the moment?

She was broke, and insurance would only cover a portion of the bakery damage, after she met her huge deductible. She was going to lose her bakery if she didn't do something fast. Her phone buzzed, drawing her attention. Dragging herself upright, Allie read the screen. *You need to make time for me, Allie. Tell me when we can meet and talk.*

She deleted the message, impressed that she could move her finger that fast. The more she indulged Blake, the more he'd bug her. In the six months since they'd been broken up, she found that ignoring him made him go away faster. She had no interest in knowing why he wanted to talk. He lived in another town now and was blessedly out of her life. He was a class-A loser, but she supposed that's what she got for rushing into a relationship with him. Everything about their romance had gone way too fast, and she'd allowed it because she was tired of being alone. What a mistake.

She wanted a partner, a wedding, a family of her own. All of that. But not with Blake. He'd waited until the newness of their relationship had worn off to show his true rude, temperamental, selfish personality. Not only was he an asshole, but he was also a terrible lover with a baby-size dick—strange for a bear shifter. She'd always imagined them hung like the proverbial horse. Worse than his unfortunate dick size was his unwillingness to do anything to please her in lieu of it. She'd faked more orgasms with Blake than Donald Trump did tans.

She blew a stray curl out of her eyes and groaned again.

Allie wiggled her left ring finger. It was naked for a reason. Many reasons if you asked Blake. He was never shy about reminding her of her shortcomings, hence the impetus for her stupid, self-depreciating list: She worked too much. She was too opinionated. She had too much debt and not enough savings. She wasn't punctual enough. She always needed help with something. She wore ugly shoes. And now, she had a ruined business.

No wonder he'd publicly and very loudly rejected her at the wedding of a mutual friend. No better place to dump someone, right?

Enough of this! Allie slipped an old apron over her head. There was too much work to be done to wallow. The bakery was closed until the end of the week so she could get some basic repairs done; hopefully enough to reopen for business until the rest could be fixed. She'd drawn a cutesy sign on the chalkboard stand outside by the door explaining the bakery had suffered some damage and wasn't offering treats, but customers could step in for free coffee. It was the least she could do for her loyal customers.

Bells chimed above the front door as it opened and let in a waft of warm, June breeze.

"Here's a frozen coffee thing with extra, why-even-bother, low-fat, non-dairy whip cream for you, Allie-bear."

Her dad, Benjamin, pushed the service door open with his hip so he could walk through, and set a tall paper cup on the glass counter for her. "Contractor will be here soon." His face scrunched as he motioned to the empty bakery cases below. "I can hardly stand not seeing yummy stuff in there."

Allie gave a sad nod of agreement. This was the first time the bakery had unexpectedly closed in three years. "I'm going to be up three days straight to get merchandise made... wait, did you say *contractor?*"

"Yep." Ben took a drink of his coffee. "Came highly recommended. He's one of them bear shifters, so you know he'll be a good worker."

Allie shifted her weight in annoyance. Since her dad had retired from his teaching job at the local high school, he's had his hands way too deep in her business. Literally and figuratively. He knew damn well that she was calling around to find a qualified contractor... okay, maybe she was stalling to avoid the high cost. But a bear-shifter? Please. Yes, they had reputations as excellent, moral businessmen. But her dad knew how Blake could get and why Allie shied away from shifters.

She wanted to speak her mind but tempered herself. He was, as usual, just trying to help.

"Dad, we talked about this."

"You've worked too hard to let –" His attention diverted to the large front window facing the street. Something had caught his eye outside. His complexion paled, his upper lip curling in distaste. "I'm disappearing now, and I was never here. Ok?"

She whipped him a look as he slinked into the back, turning to wink at her before he disappeared beyond the double kitchen doors. Curious what had scared him off, she looked back to the windows and saw a familiar pink form walking briskly past. Allie grimaced and whispered a chant. "Please don't come in, please don't come in, please don't... damn, damn, damn."

The bells jingled, the bells from hell. She really should have locked the door instead of welcoming customers in for coffee. Plastering on a smile, she straightened at the counter and smoothed the apron over her purple high-low skirt.

"Morning, Marybeth." Her tone came out pleasing enough though inside, she was fighting the urge to jump off a cliff. Her mama had always said, if you don't feel it, fake it. Rest her soul, she'd be proud.

Marybeth Dawson gasped and did a three-sixty, taking in the bakery's state with a gaped mouth.

"Oh my God, Allie Mae, what happened in here?"

"Tornado. Came clear through."

Marybeth dragged a shocked look to Allie, her hand going to her chest. "A tornado in *Estes Park, Colorado?*"

Allie's face hurt from trying not to laugh. Instead, she kept the smile in place and took a breath through her nose. Marybeth was MB in Allie's mind: Mega Bitch, and it wouldn't be long before the ex-Mayor's wife started living up to the moniker. Marybeth broke out of her stupor and approached the counter. She placed one hand with perfectly pink fingernails on the top and began to drum them like the claws they were. Claws she wanted to sink into Benjamin Rowe in the worst possible way.

"I saw Benny come in. Where is he?"

Benny. Jesus Christ. The man was sixty-two years old and built like a brick shit house.

"I'm afraid he's already left. Is there something I can help you with?"

Marybeth gave a dismissive chuckle. "Yes, I'd like to speak to Benny and I'm sure you know just where to find him."

He's eagerly hiding in hell along with the bells above my door.

"I'm not sure where he went. He left his cell phone behind, as usual."

Allie slowly pulled a phone from her apron pocket, not caring that it was hers and not her dad's. Like MB would know. Except that she always seemed to know everything, about everyone, before they even knew it themselves. She was the Queen of Everyone's Damn Business— her father's words— and heaven help you if you didn't give the woman what she wanted. She had no qualms about sticking some dirty business on you and letting the town know about it, true or not.

Marybeth's bubblegum claws walked over to the extra coffee cup sitting close to Allie's. Allie winced a little. Shit.

"Darling, I know business isn't good enough that you need *two* cups of coffee to keep up. I mean, look at this shithole. I heard wild animals did a number on the place, but seriously."

Allie cleared her throat and slid her father's coffee toward her cup. She snaked both cups off the counter and put them on the table by the register, hoping that when she turned back around, Pink Powderpuff would be gone. The drum of pointed tips on glass said otherwise.

"Oh, I don't know. I think the ripping and shredding and destruction add a little something special to the place, don't you?"

"You know Allie Mae, I'm here to place a rather large order of things for my moonlight garden party, and it would be prudent of you to watch yourself. Or I might have to go down the street to Bella Blu and see what they'll do for me."

Oh, I couldn't be so lucky, Allie thought. She glanced at the waded-up bank note on the floor by her feet and clenched her jaw. Marybeth's moonlight party was a big deal. Half of Estes Park and Denver came— well, anyone with money, basically.

Bella Blu was a hundred-year-old cornerstone and was always getting the bigger orders. Competing with the well-known bakery was hard as hell. And she needed the cash.

"What do you have in mind?"

Marybeth smiled wide, causing the powder on her face to crack into her laugh lines. "Well, I'm not sure. I'm thinking some petit fours, and those decadent lemon cupcakes with the pink frosting."

"Raspberry frosting."

"Mmmm-hmm. Delightful. However, I'd only be able to place an order of, say, two hundred to start if Benny were available to escort me for the evening."

Allie drew in a breath through her nose and forced her expression to stay relaxed. Her dad had been very clear to Marybeth that he wasn't interested in her advances, yet the widow pursued Ben like he was the very breath she needed to live. It would have been kind of sweet if she weren't so creepy in her persistence.

"I can't really speak for my father, Marybeth. But I'll be sure to let him know."

The older woman looked Allie up and down before she turned away. "You do that."

Allie let out a breath, waiting for the woman to leave. But right before she got to the door, MB stopped and glanced up. She pointed above the window and turned to Allie with a disgusted expression.

"Allie Mae, what on earth is *that?*"

Allie cocked her head to see better. A long, thin, blackish line settled in the crease where the wall met the ceiling.

"Is that... is that *mold?*" The older woman gasped.

A cold chill went over her spine. No, no, no. The universe wouldn't be that horrible, would it?

MB and her huge, gossipy mouth would tell everyone that Sticky Sweet was contaminated or something. She was already up to her eyeballs in debt trying to keep this place open; she couldn't afford to lose business. She grappled for something to say that would hold Marybeth off, but nothing came to mind.

Jesus, what else could go wrong today?

"Allie?" The woman demanded.

"It's... it's just..."

A loud sound came from the ceiling, making Allie jump. Pausing at the unfamiliar noise, she listened to the patter and creak coming from above. It got louder, like something rolling or running from one side of the ceiling to another. A sinking feeling welled in her middle. Holy shit, what was that?

Suddenly, a loud pop burst through the air. Allie cried out as the sprinkler system let loose and cold water rained down. Her arms went out in shock, her mouth a frozen, "O." Marybeth screamed and ran out the door, hollering something about her silk blouse and a lawsuit.

Still in shock, Allie slowly covered her head with her hands as if to stave off the torrent. Water pooled on the floor and bounced off the display cases. The walls began to darken with moisture.

Anger welled in her chest and bubbled out her throat in a garbled cry. "Great! Just one more thing to add to the Loser Allie List, damn it!"

That's it. She couldn't take another complication. Wiping her face, she tried to remember where the control was for the sprinkler system when a shadow blocked the doorway that Marybeth's panicked exit had left wide open.

Allie blinked. Once. Twice.

A man large enough to take up nearly the entire doorframe stood inside getting pelted by the spray. Instead of consternation, he had a look of pure enjoyment on his face as if he were out frolicking in the rain instead of standing under a torrent. Dark hair slicked against his head and curled at the base of his neck. His red tee shirt slowly plastered by degrees to his body, revealing dips and lines of muscle and perfectly structured anatomy, inch by inch.

Her mouth fell open, suddenly glad for the cold water to cool the flush that heated her skin.

Allie forgot to breathe.

He smiled and ran a hand over his forehead to push back his hair. Sky-blue eyes bored into hers, their corners crinkled with humor, his smile falling to a cocky grin.

"Staring costs extra, sweetheart."

Chapter Two

♥

Well, well, well. This job just might not suck ass after all.

Dax Mitchell roved the hot little blonde with an eager gaze. His heart did an odd flip-flop thing and banged hard against his chest. Huh. Must be the coolness of the water beating down on him, making his adrenaline surge.

She had a pin-up body if he ever saw one. The tie of the apron around her waist gave her a perfect hourglass figure, the rise of her plump breasts pushing against the top. The water? Hell yeah, it soaked the thin fabric, making it cling to those perfect mounds even more. Her left upper arm was covered with a tattoo of orange hibiscus flowers and silvery stars, and a tiny nose piercing glittered in the light.

The shifter in him couldn't look away. Both his bear and his human sides thought she was stunning.

Damn, this was a good day.

Before he could introduce himself, the woman's pretty face skewed, and she rolled her brown eyes.

"Seriously? That's the line you're going with?"

She hurried behind a set of stainless-steel doors, and he couldn't help but enjoy the sway of her hips as she went. Dax followed as far as the counter. A moment later, the sprinklers hissed, and the water trickled to a stop.

She came back out with a thick towel in one hand, placed another on the counter and began blotting her hair. Despite being wet, her hair was starting to curl at the ends.

"Can I help you?" The flat tone to her voice screamed annoyance.

Dax flashed her a smile. He was dripping a bit himself. "Got another towel?"

"No."

His eyebrows raised. "No?"

He appreciated her spunk, and honestly, it was the only reason he was still standing here. That, and the fact that his father had strong-armed him into coming. His dad loved Sticky Sweet Bakery's maple sticky buns and jumped at the chance when the bakery called for help. Mitchell Construction to the rescue, despite that they exclusively did corporate work now. Oh, the power of baked goods to help the little guy, apparently.

Her hands slapped against her hips in a helpless gesture before she tossed the extra towel at him. Dax caught it with one hand. Her expression fell as a distinctive tremble claimed her lower lip.

Oh no. Bad day... this was turning into a very bad day.

"Everything. Is. Soaked clear through." Her voice was thick and broken.

Despite the counter being between them, he took a step back. Women's tears were not his forte. He avoided female emotions at all costs unless lust was involved. That he welcomed with open arms.

"Yeah, that, uh, that sucks."

Her gaze steeled to his and her voice firmed up. "Yeah."

He took another little step back as she narrowed her eyes and came through the half door to stand beside him. He could pick her up with one arm and carry her around like a curvy little doll, but the look on her face scared the hell out of him. Bear shifter or not, being on the receiving end of a woman's emotional roll was not his idea of a good time.

"You know what else sucks? Having to send all my staff home and close my bakery for a week. Losing profits sucks. And now something made the sprinklers turn on..."

"A raccoon."

She blinked. He smiled. Well, that shut her up.

"Wh-what?"

Dax wiped stray drips of water from his face. His bear had smelled the offending rodent before he saw it. The animal inside had him churned around, begging to be let out like a dog itching to chase a squirrel up a tree.

"It's a mammal. Gray-ish, black, and white. Looks like it's wearing a cute little burglar mask. Probably ate through a wire and caused the sprinklers to default."

She cocked her head, exposing the length of her creamy white neck. "You're goddamned adorable, aren't you? Get out."

All that curly, wavy mess of hair fell over one shoulder and he had the strongest urge to run his fingers through it and pull her pink lips to his. The flash of anger in her eyes made his cock stir. Well, hello lust. Nice of you to wake up now. How could he help it? Between her kissable lips and temper, he was almost beside himself.

"Don't shoot the messenger."

"Seriously." she sighed. "Animal control just plucked two out of here the other day."

Her teeth were even and white, with one eye tooth that jutted forward with a little sass. She had the kind of skin that glowed like she'd spent hours doing whatever women did to get that effect. He wanted to cup her jaw and run his thumbs over the smooth rise of her cheeks, feel all that satiny skin under his fingers.

With a mental shake, Dax drew himself back to the moment.

"I saw one climbing out of your little attic window before I came in."

She slumped against the counter; one hip braced at the edge. Dax slowly ran the towel over his hair. His clothes were starting to cling, and thank all the gods, so were hers. Humidity was taking over, creating a stifling atmosphere. They needed to get some windows open and fans going. With that thought, he looked around the room, easily spotting the reason he'd been called here. She wasn't kidding; the critters had done a number on the place. She'd mentioned being closed a few days. He didn't have the heart to tell her it might be longer than that.

"This is a historic building," she mumbled. Dax focused his sharp hearing to better pick up her low tone. "I paid a mint for this place so it wouldn't get torn down. It was fine, *fine*, when I bought it! I mean, besides the electrical fire."

Dax ran the towel down his forearms. She looked at him then, followed the movement of the towel.

"Electrical fire?" He prompted.

She ran her top teeth over her lower lip as he dragged the towel up his bicep. His sleeve went up with it, baring flesh and muscle. "Uh, yeah... and the explosion."

Dax moved to his other arm with a little grin. She was completely transfixed on what he was doing, and he loved it. Nothing wrong with some female appreciation, even if she did seem like a handful.

"Explosion."

"Mmm-hmm. It was minor, unlike the drug bust."

He dropped the towel. She drew back, her eyes snapping up to his like he'd broken some trance. Dax shook his head.

"*Drug* bust?"

With a sigh, she untied the apron and whipped it over her head. Motioning above the front windows, she then crossed her arms.

"Is that mold?" Her eyes went wide, her mouth parting. "I keep an immaculate kitchen. You could lick the floor and still kiss your mama, I swear."

Dax grinned. "I'm not the health department, sweetheart."

"Who *are* you?"

Your mate.

The words slammed into Dax's mind and scurried off, but not without stunning him. All his family's warnings about him having one last chance to take a mate were clouding his psyche, that's all. How many times can a guy hear his father hollering, "You're going to die, cub-less and alone!" before his brain starts putting that shit on repeat?

Yes, he needed a mate. No, he wasn't in a hurry to find one. Except that he had one week to find a mate or his biological ability to produce cubs, and his epic virility, would be gone. His clock was literally ticking away and yet, he had no huge sense of urgency to do anything about it. No matter how hard he tried, he couldn't get himself to care that he'd be cub-less and alone. He'd do what he wanted, thank you.

Extending a hand, he didn't wait for the woman to take it. He took hers instead. "Dax Mitchell, your contractor, Ms. Rowe."

She didn't pull away as he expected. And he was glad. Her hand was small and warm in his. The press of her soft skin against his palm drove electric sparks up his arm. Without pre-thought, he rubbed his thumb over her knuckles, once, twice. Never actually shaking her hand, just holding it.

"I didn't hire you."

She looked up at him, her fingers moving softly against his palm. Dax took a step closer. He was tall enough that he could easily curl around her, envelop her body in his. Protect her.

"Look around. You really want to let me go?"

The thought of leaving drummed up an uneasy feeling. Her eyes searched his and he had the impression she was considering booting him out the door. He knew a hopeless expression when he saw one and it was splashed all over her tantalizing face.

"What's the point? I have raccoons, mold, and probably water damage now. The list keeps growing."

The flatness of Allie's tone made it seem as if she were talking about something beyond just getting this place fixed. He vaguely remembered something she'd said about a Loser Allie List as he'd walked in. Sounded like a woman being way too hard on herself. Or... someone else being hard on her. The protective surge blossomed in his breast again.

"Hey, it's nothing I can't fix."

Allie pulled away then and his hand felt immediately empty. She went behind the counter to the doors that lead to the back. "Look, I can't afford you. Now if you'll excuse me, I need to call a few friends to help me dry this place out."

Well, fuck. She was kicking him out. She pushed the doors and was almost through when he called her name. She paused but didn't turn around.

"Allie, we'll work something out."

He meant it. The urge to help her, no, the *need*, was all-consuming and confusing. Damn it, he didn't need this complication right now.

The mating ceremony was next week, something he had to endure and possibly use to find a mate. Life was a tangled mess and Allie Rowe was going to be a rose branch with thorns to make it worse.

She gave him a quick backward glance. "Get your tight, wet shirt and sexy muscles out of here. I'll get a few friends to help me dry this place out, and you stop by about eight tomorrow morning, and we'll talk."

Oooh, the sass was back.

"Yes, ma'am."

"Damn right," she said, and disappeared behind the doors with a sway of her hips he'd be thinking about all fucking night.

Chapter Three

♥

Getting a few friends in to help dry out the bakery turned out to be unnecessary after a three-person restoration crew showed up a couple of hours after Dax left. When she'd tried to protest that she hadn't hired them, she was given a receipt that showed the service was paid in full. Anonymously. By late afternoon, they had everything moved, aired out, dried, and put back together. They'd left three big fans running with the promise to be back to get them. Luckily, all the commotion hadn't produced any new raccoons.

When she'd returned to Sticky Sweet this morning, the atmosphere felt better inside. Spirits a bit lifted, she decided to do a little baking. More from desire than necessity at this point.

Allie wiped her forehead on her sleeve to get rid of the flour dust tickling her face, and then put all her frustration into rolling out cookie dough.

There was no question that Dax Mitchell was behind hiring and paying for the restoration crew. As grateful as she was, all Allie could see was dollar signs. And a fair amount of red. She'd never authorized him to send anyone over. It occurred to her that she didn't even have his number so she could call and chew his ass.

What a nice ass it would be to chew on.

She flushed all over just thinking about Dax's huge body taking up the entire doorframe. He'd been a delicious mix of arrogant sassiness and sweetness, and hot! Lord was that man hot.

Her experience with shifters was limited to her relationship with Blake. Except for their size, it was almost impossible to tell a shifter from a regular human at first glance. For the most part, they kept to their own, preferring to mingle among their own communities in the mountainous area. The shifter men from the Estes Park pack seemed so cocky and full of themselves—all proud of their muscles and alpha swagger, trying to impress her as she filled white bakery bags with cookies and rolls.

Her upper lip curled. Then again, the human men she'd dated had all turned out to be wrong too.

Dax might have one big selling point though. No way would that man have a small dick.

Her face went hot. She looked around as if her friend Becks could have heard her thoughts, but she was asleep on a stool in the corner in true narcoleptic fashion.

Allie squirmed a little and wiped a hand over her forehead. She'd had some crazy reaction to the man, for sure. All it took was his eyes on her, and her latent sex drive came alive. Wrap her legs around that man's tasty hips and grind herself into oblivion? Yes, please!

"What's that look on your face?"

Her dad turned with a large metal tray in his oven-mitted hands. She, Becks, and her dad had come in at five a.m. to start cleaning, but Becks' narcolepsy medications had been recently changed and her need for a nap found her on the stool with her head in her hands. Allie pulled her dad into the back to help make a few dozen cookies and some other treats. What good was a bakery without sweets? Even a ruined bakery closed to customers had to be filled with a tantalizing aroma, if nothing else, to remind Allie why she put so much of her heart and soul into this place.

She inspected the sheet of chocolate chip toffee cookies before indicating he should put them on the racks. He couldn't bake to save his life, but he was a great right-hand man.

"That look would be consternation over how to pay the contractor you hired."

Ben smiled wide. "Ah, nice young man, huh? So brawny."

She chuckled. Brawny, yes. Yes, yes, yes. "He's a shifter, dad. They're usually pretty brawny. And you know how I feel about them."

"One bitter cup of coffee doesn't mean every cup will be nasty." Her dad returned to the commercial oven for another tray of cookies. "He's single too. I asked. My radar isn't bad this time, sweetheart; I promise."

She rolled her eyes. Always optimistic about her love life, her dad wasn't shy about steering her toward men he thought were suitable. Too bad his taste sucked.

"Speaking of single and bad radar, Marybeth is in heat and getting a little aggressive about it." She side-eyed Ben, whose smile had fallen into a worried expression she hadn't seen where Marybeth was concerned before. She was an annoyance, but maybe more?

Ben silently filled the cookie racks and Allie turned back to the tray of sticky buns she'd made earlier. A few minutes of silence passed, and she couldn't take it anymore.

"Something I should know about Marybeth, dad?"

"Not really. She found me after the sprinkler incident yesterday and filled my ears with her high-pitched, hurt-your-head voice. You know the one, 'Benjamin Rowe, your daughter tried to drown me after I offered her my business, and I might just have to ask for damages to replace my blouse because of the water damage. It's three-hundred dollars, ruined'."

"Three hundred dollars," Allie gushed in disbelief. Marybeth's late husband had left her way too much money.

"She made me a deal." Ben's voice was heavy with regret. "I took it to save you from having to pay up. And she promised to still place an order for her party."

Allie wiped her hands on her apron and turned to her dad with a furrowed brow. "Tell me you didn't make a deal with that troll."

The oven timers dinged, and Ben turned to take out the baking sheets.

"It's nothing serious. I'll just escort her to the party, that's all." Before she could argue, he held up a hand and gave her his stern look, which was more sympathetic puppy than firm father. "She also promised not to sue, whatever that means."

"It's her classic threat. You know that."

Rustling from the corner signaled that Becks had roused from her nap. The stool wiggled as she bolted from leaning against the counter to sitting. "I'm here," she announced groggily as if she'd just arrived. Rubbing her eyes, she looked around with narrowed eyes. "Wait, how did I get here?"

Allie ruffled her friend's dark brown hair. "You spent the night at my house, and I drove here, you lunatic. I don't think these new meds are working for you, honey."

Ben nodded in agreement just as a knock came from the front door. Allie looked at the overhead clock. It was just after six a.m., and she hadn't yet opened the front door. Quickly wiping her hands with a towel, she headed to the front of the bakery. The familiar click and pop of the front door lock being turned stopped her in her tracks.

Chills raced down her arms as she hurriedly turned on the light switch and flooded the area in golden light.

Dax groaned and rubbed his eyes with one hand.

"What the hell are you doing here?" Allie demanded. Her heart jumped, but it wasn't from being startled. Dax's huge arms were bare, the gray tee shirt he wore cut off at the sleeves and clinging to his chest. No water required this time to mold it to his perfect body. His blonde hair was tucked behind his ears, the ends curling at the base of his neck.

He held up a single key on a ring and spun it around his finger. "Your dad gave me this so I could start as early as I like."

"Oh, wonderful."

He grinned wide, showing off the divot in the center of his chin. "Something smells really good."

Allie cocked one side of her mouth. "That would be the scent of my despair."

"Your despair smells exactly like chocolate chip cookies."

Dax made a slow saunter around the room, perusing the space with a practiced eye. Jeans clung to the round rise of his ass and gripped the length of powerful thighs. Shifters might be cocky asshats, but she couldn't deny this one was sexy as hell.

"Remember what I said about staring?"

Dax's voice startled her. Allie's face heated as he gave her a slow glance over his shoulder. She wet her lips and squared her shoulders. Her fingers actually itched to caress the rise of his ass.

"Add it to my tab, I suppose. Seems the bill's already getting high, thanks to the restoration crew you sent over."

He nodded, pleased. And completely ignoring her sarcasm. "They did a nice job. It looks very dry in here."

Rolling her eyes, Allie turned to go into the back. She needed to keep her interactions with Dax to a minimum. The pulse in her temple was pounding and her chest was tight with irritation. She was doing everything possible to ignore the needy ache between her legs.

Ben looked at her in question when she resumed her spot at the counter and picked up a rolling pin.

"Contractor is here," she muttered, and began rolling the last of the almond sugar cookies. "We need to finish up these cookies and get busy tidying up the store."

"Oh, good. I told him to come as early as he liked. Gave him a key."

"Let's just finish up here, okay?" A thought popped into her mind. "When did you see Dax to give him the key?"

"We had a beer together at the Wild last night. Nice young man. He's, uh, single."

Allie set the rolling pin down a little too hard. "I know, you already told me. Maybe *you* should date him."

"Sorry, I'm not into dudes."

Dax walked close to the butcherblock counter where she was working, so silent that he could have been standing there this entire time and she wouldn't have known. He nodded to her father in that bromance way guys had, and her dad nodded back as if he were forty years younger and wearing his ballcap backwards. Her skin began to heat, her nerves becoming a chaotic mess as Dax stood beside her.

Becks opened her eyes from the chair she was slouched in, blinked. Blinked again and then raised her hand. "I'll date him."

Ben snickered. "Honey, you can't stay awake long enough to handle a man like this."

"Dad!" Allie cried.

"I'm up for it. Allie, make some strong coffee and go get an illegal Ritalin from that kid down the street." Becks moved to slip off her chair, but Allie stopped her with an amused wave. Her friend's seizure disorder and narcolepsy might technically render her, 'disabled,' but Becks took her illnesses in stride with good humor.

Dax turned to Allie, and everyone else in the room seemed to disappear.

"Want to give me a tour so I can check out the plumbing, electrical systems, and the general layout?"

Breaking from his gaze, she cut the dough with a flower-shaped cookie cutter, not bothering to look at him. "Dad can show you."

Dax leaned over with one elbow on the counter so he could peer directly at her face. His voice was low, the whispered timber of it making her nipples perk.

"I thought you owned this place."

"I do."

"You're not acting like it. You want daddy to make decisions for your business?"

They locked gazes. Dax's was too self-satisfied. She wanted to wipe that look right off his face. Or lick. Or kiss. Anger and irritation and for fuck's sake, a helping of lust, filled her completely. How dare he imply she wasn't capable or willing to run her own damn business. She'd had enough of men always doubting her.

Allie continued cutting the last row of cookies without taking her eyes off Dax. Her dad rushed over and took the cutter from her hand. "I'll finish these up. I know, I know, 350 degrees for ten minutes and not a minute longer."

"Fine," Allie said and untied her apron. Whipping it over her head and dumping it on the counter, she turned. "This way."

She wasn't going to let this sexy brute get under her skin, or anything else. Allie walked briskly to the back hallway that led to the storage and refrigeration rooms. Looking up where the raccoons had damaged part of the ceiling, she gasped. Huge brown circles coated the remaining ceiling tiles. Damn, the sprinkler.

Dax nudged her along, as if to prevent her from dwelling on the ceiling.

She responded by walking into the storage room. The critters hadn't made it to this room, luckily, and the sprinkler system was never installed in here. A sense of pride filled her when she stepped in, as always. The room was carefully and meticulously organized, the bright pink walls cheery, and the custom oak shelving lined with coordinated fabric baskets. Boxes and plastic tubs all sat in their places, along with extra baking trays, bowls, and other equipment. This room mimicked the customer area of the bakery, the pink and yellow colors, and black and white damask fabrics exactly the way Allie had pictured for the bakery when she'd bought it. She'd put a year's worth of work into this place before she opened for business. No way was she going to let normal maintenance issues bring her down.

Afraid to look up, but doing it anyway, her heart sank at the same water spots dotting the ceiling as in the hallway. She'd thought this room had gone unscathed.

"Oh no."

Dax put a big hand on her shoulder and gave a light squeeze. She whipped a look where he touched her, her body humming at his touch.

"This is fixable. Okay? Don't worry." He gave a sympathetic smile and drew his hand away. Allie involuntarily leaned toward him; her body not ready to give up the delicious contact. How did she fail to notice how good he smelled? Like pine and outdoors and clean, fresh soap. More delicious than the scent of her despair. Maybe it was his scent, or his touch, or both, but she felt comforted. Some of the tension left her shoulders, and the ache behind her left temple went away.

Dax's eyes fell to her lips, and she really noticed how sculpted and soft his mouth was. Those lips were made for trailing a woman's body, for kissing secret places, for...

He abruptly moved away and headed back to the hall. He was walking into the second kitchen area when she caught up with him.

"What's this?" He asked, looking around.

Her heart was still racing from his proximity in the other room. "It's a secondary kitchen I had put in so I can produce gluten-free baked goods. All the recipes have been developed and tested, but I'm waiting on certification before I start offering them."

His face twisted a bit. "Gluten-free? That's no flour, right?"

Allie was used to having to explain it. Her mother had had celiac disease, making it dangerous for her to eat wheat, barley, or rye because of the gluten content.

"Well, wheat flour. That's part of it. Gluten-free foods is a huge industry. I've done a lot of research and I think starting up a dedicated product line that can be shipped all over the US will be good for my bottom line. Anyway, it's a work in progress." And it was something Bella Blu wasn't already doing.

Dax seemed to roll that around in his head for a moment before he turned to fully face her.

"You know," he whispered. Allie realized just how far he'd leaned into her. His breath touched her face, minty and hot. "Your dad is right. You should go on a date with me."

"He... he never said that."

Get with it, Allie! She gave herself a mental shake and shuffled a step back. Not because she didn't want Dax this close, but because she was *this close* to throwing herself into his arms. What was wrong with her? She'd never had such a fast and deep reaction to a man. None of her exes had brought about this kind of want in her. The want to be taken, to do naughty, dirty things. The want to be taken so hard she'd feel Dax for a week afterward.

"He implied it." He trapped his lower lip under his top teeth before wetting his lips with the tip of his tongue.

"Lots of things have been implied today." Like her body implying that Dax's gesture of comfort made him suitable enough to have hot monkey sex with... even though he'd just hurt her in the end, like everyone else. He'd find something to add to the Loser Allie List.

Worse, he was a shifter. What if his temper was as unpredictable and hot as Blake's? A slight shudder rolled over her body. No way was she putting herself in the path of a man like that again. She was taking her next relationship slow and give it time to develop true colors before she fully committed.

"Go out with me."

She took another small step backwards, Blake's anger-filled eyes on her mind.

"I'm not interested." She crossed her arms over her full breasts to ensure he didn't see how her nipples pressed against her shirt. Traitorous boobs.

"That's a shame."

Before she could respond, he asked her to show him the access to the attic, and he disappeared into it, all traces of playboy Dax gone. She looked after him a moment, expecting he'd pop back down and make some comment about trying to convince her. He didn't.

Allie swallowed and walked back to the kitchen. She and Dax needed to be strictly professional. She wasn't looking for another moody shifter or damn heartbreak!

So why did she feel so disappointed?

Her cell phone buzzed from her back pocket. Pulling it out, she peered at the screen. *Allie.*

One word. Just one. As she read it, Blake's flat, warning tone of voice filled her mind. It was the tone he used specifically to say her name when he was displeased or upset with her. She shuddered and put the phone away.

She thought she was past the days of being afraid of her own name.

Chapter Four

♥

Dax inspected the plumbing and took samples of the black stuff from above the window. He made a point to stay out of Allie's way while he worked. That woman did something to him, and her refusal to go out with him only made it worse. What guy didn't want a challenge? Her voice had a cautious undertone when she'd turned him down, as if she were rejecting him on autopilot instead of giving it any real thought.

If she really wasn't interested, fine. He wouldn't bring it up again. But if she was trying to tiptoe into a maybe-yes, he'd push a little. There was a fine line between pursuit and being a creep and he'd never want to make her uncomfortable. But damn, the way she looked at him when she didn't think he was paying attention made it easy to think she was, at least a little bit, interested. Not that it should matter. He never had a lack of women vying for his attention. Lately, his father and brothers have been digging up women left and right, trying to pressure him into picking one.

The problem was, not a single woman he'd been with or met had been The One. He'd been attracted to his exes, of course. They'd had fun in and out of bed. But to commit a lifetime to any of them? No way. Some had been more interested in his family money than him. Others just weren't mother and wife material.

He hadn't felt that *spark*, that *need,* and *want* for more with any of them. But Allie did something different to him—gave him an antsy electricity that he couldn't control. Whatever it was, he wanted to explore it further. If only his clock wasn't winding down. But it was, and he didn't have time to explore anything.

In a handful of days, he'd be forced take a mate or lose his manhood.

He slipped out the back door and walked around front where he'd parked his truck. A group of people were gathered in front of Sticky Sweet, arms crossed as they chatted in disappointed tones about the bakery being closed. Those must be some amazing maple sticky buns if Allie could attract a crowd like this, plus enamor his father with her baking.

His cell phone rang just as he pulled up to the health department to drop off the samples.

"Hey dad," he said as he jumped out of the truck.

"Yeah, you going to come help chop wood tonight for the Pairing Festival?"

His dad wasn't really asking a question. He was telling Dax to show up tonight. Dax waited for traffic and jogged across the street. "Yes, sir. I'll be there."

"Good. Half a cord yet to split. Hopefully, it'll be enough."

The Pairing happened every three years on the brightest full moon of summer. Shifter packs from all over Colorado and surrounding states came to find a mate. His family was hosting the festival this time around on one-hundred acres of land. His father had the perfect spot which offered a mixture of woods and a four-acre spot of grassland where the bonfires would be.

Each six-foot-wide fire circle offered a place for mingling, conversation and hopefully, pairing up.

"We'll cut extra, just in case."

Rowan Mitchell cleared his throat and Dax took a deep breath. He knew what was coming next.

"You're the oldest of my sons. You have an example to set for your brothers. How's it going to look if you're mating age passes and what? You'll never produce a cub from your loins."

"Dad," Dax interjected. "Come on. My loins? Really?"

"I mean it."

Dax stood outside the Health Department door, wishing this conversation were over. But he knew better than to hurry his father. Rowan had built a construction business from the ground up and was one of the most successful corporate contractors in the tri-state area. Among shifters, his very name brought respect. He'd helped govern the Estes Park pack for sixty years and was a respected Alpha leader among the bear shifters. He'd passed his Alpha genes to his sons and now, Dax was obligated to do the same.

"Yes, sir." Dax knew nothing he said would satisfy his dad. "I'm — "

"I was going to wait to tell you this, but there's no point in waiting anymore. You take a mate at the Pairing, or you're out of the business. It's come to this, Dax. Your playboying around has done nothing but bring you within days of losing your ability to mate. Family is everything and you're not going to have one because of your dicking around."

Dax clenched his eyes and rubbed his temple. "You're cutting me out?"

"I will."

Tension rolled down Dax's spine, anger flaring within him. "I haven't found anyone I want." Not entirely true. "You'd rather I settle for someone I don't want just to see me mated?"

There was a pause and Dax hoped his dad had come to his senses. How was it fair he was expected to pair bond for the sake of reproduction and not, well, love?

"Yes." Short. Simple. "I know it's not what your mother would have wanted, but you've left me no choice."

With that, his father hung up. Dax stared at the phone for a minute, trying to get a grip on his emotions. His mother wouldn't want this, no. She'd rather settle for no grandcubs than watch her oldest son bonded to a mate he didn't love. Damn the human cancer that had taken her too soon. Emotion pricked at his eyes, but he forced it back.

He was first heir to the Mitchell Corporation. He wanted a family of his own. He wanted a partner for life. More, he wanted those things with someone he actually loved. Why wasn't love coming easily so he could just get on with it?

Frustrated, Dax went inside and dropped off the samples, then drove to the contractor supply store to drop off a materials list for the bakery. His head ached and his body felt too tense. When he made it back to Sticky Sweet, he was wound tight and ready for a beer or an orgasm to help him relax. Both. He could go home and give himself both.

Right, as if he had nothing better to do.

Using the front door, Dax stepped inside Sticky Sweet. Amazing smells of sugar and frosting and baked deliciousness filled his nose and immediately relaxed him. His stomach rumbled quietly, and he realized he'd never tried anything from this bakery before. He'd driven past it how many times over the years but had never thought to stop. Allie had been inside—waiting—all this time.

An odd feeling captured him. They'd probably passed each other in town; eaten at the same restaurants, gone to the same stores. Yet not once had his primal senses gone off to draw him to her. His mating radar hadn't led him to her. But these feelings he had when he was with her were strong enough to make him believe she could be his mate.

So... why hadn't he found her until now?

Becks stood on a ladder, hanging curtains over the big front windows. She smiled at him as he walked in.

"What if you fall asleep up there? Then you'll fall and sue me." Allie's voice called out from somewhere nearby.

Becks didn't take her eyes off Dax.

"Narcolepsy doesn't work that way, smart one. Besides, there's a really hot guy right here who will have no problem catching me."

Allie popped up from behind the counter, her hair spilling out in bobbing curls around the purple handkerchief she had tied around her head. Her cheeks were pink, her lips shiny with clear gloss that made them look plump and inviting. A dimple curved into her right cheek as she smiled at a customer and his heart beat faster.

Had she looked this glow-y this morning? It was hard to tell because she was pretty no matter what, but his ego thought maybe she'd prettied up for him.

The fucking urge to blow a load got worse. Forget the beer. He just wanted Allie. Under him, her legs wrapped around him while he drove into her; hearing her scream his name until he fucked them both into exhaustion. Then he'd hold her close and run his fingers through that beautiful hair and fall asleep to the weight of her head on his chest, over his heart.

It took all his will not to rush at her, throw her over his shoulder and carry her off like a true shifter male should. Good thing he was feeling more human than animal today, though that was quickly beginning to change.

She held a paper coffee cup between her hands as she appraised him across the space. A muscle in her jaw twitched; her pupils going round and big. The warmth of her scent increased, making his pulse quicken and his urges to get stronger. She was reacting to him in a very base way—her body saying loudly what it wanted, what it needed, without voicing a word.

A sweet breeze blew in from the propped-open front door. It was a perfect day, warm and sunny, to take Allie to the woods. To show her what a true shifter male could do to her body, to her heart.

Becks cleared her throat as the sound of high heels clicking on the brick floor filled the room. A woman brushed past him as she came inside, not paying him a bit of attention as she beelined it to Allie.

Allie's hands tightened around the cup and Dax thought she might crush it. The women began to speak in hushed tones; Allie doing more listening than speaking, as the other woman went on and on in a high-pitched voice that grated over his skin.

Becks came slowly down the ladder. She seemed a bit unsteady. Dax rushed to place a hand on her lower back until she'd touched the ground.

She nodded toward Allie. "This won't be good. MB has had it out for Allie as long as I can remember."

"MB?"

Becks whispered. "Mega Bitch, Mighty Bitchy, Massive Butthole... you get the idea."

Allie's face was tense, and it raised a red flag in him to intervene. He held back, knowing it wasn't his place. This time.

Dax picked up the older woman's unhappy tones and homed in his primal hearing to the sound. She was dressed all in pink with fingernails to match, which she drummed impatiently on the countertop.

Curious, Dax moved closer.

"I'd love to give you an order for a hundred more, Allie Mae, but I'm not sure you're responsible enough to handle that many. I mean, just look what you did to my clothes the other day."

"It's up to you Marybeth. I'm happy to make as many as you like."

"Yes, well. I've already checked prices at Bella Blu. Perhaps you'll want to price match?"

Allie's chest moved with a tight breath. "I'm afraid I can't go any lower on the price. But I will need you to decide today. I need to get started immediately to fill an order that big in time."

Without taking her eyes off the woman, Allie reached below the counter and produced a black coffee mug. She popped the top off the paper coffee cup and slowly poured steaming brew into the other mug. White lettering on the side said, 'Tears of my enemies.' She lifted the mug with the words clearly visible to her customer while she took a sip.

Dax grinned.

The woman shifted her weight and sighed again. "Can you even complete my order in this disaster?" She waved a hand around the room. "Is it even sanitary?"

Pinkie didn't wait for a response as she took a slip of paper from her purse, slapped it on the counter and eyed Allie's mug. "I swear Allie Mae; your manners are the reason you can't get a man. *This* is the final list. You need to come down on price. Come on now, I know you need the money. Take my damn business. I'm doing you a massive favor."

Dax narrowed his eyes. Who was this bitch? It didn't matter. He was putting an end to this right now. He flung the service door open, startling both women. Without preamble, he moved behind the counter and stood beside Allie. The woman looked him up... way up, and then back down, her eyes staying on his chest a little too long. Allie's lips parted but she didn't say anything.

"I've an order to place. Two hundred of whatever she ordered, at full price. And lots of maple sticky buns. We'll figure out how many."

He whipped out a checkbook and put it on the counter directly in front of the woman, whose mouth now gaped to the extent the powder on her face cracked into little lines around her lips.

"What on earth would you need with lemon lavender cupcakes, young man?"

Dax snorted, then grinned when the woman made a disgusted face. "Lemon lavender? No thanks. I was thinking... you know, dark choco-late...with..."

"Bacon." Allie said, crossing her arms. "You want chocolate stout cupcakes, filled with salted caramel cream, and topped with dark choco-late and bacon-dotted frosting."

Hell yeah, he did.

He looked at Allie. Hunger rolled through him, deep and insistent, but not for food. "Can I have one right now? Make it two. Three." He'd take a bite in between luscious nibbles and kisses over her delicate skin.

The corner of her mouth twitched, and her eyes lit up like stars. "Sorry, big guy."

"You said bacon, right?"

"Yes."

"Is it like smoked bacon, or thick cut, or Applewood, or —? "

She grinned and his heart jumped to see it.

"It's just bacon.'

'It's never *just* bacon."

She grinned. "Whatever you want."

Was it just his imagination, or did her eyes darken when she said that? If only she knew what he wanted. "Sold." Dax leaned in a little closer and caught a whiff of coconut and flowers. "Let's make a test batch. We'll have a private tasting later."

If he had his way, he'd be tasting every inch of her curvy body.

Allie's lips moved as if she was going to reply, but a loud crack coming from the other side of the counter made them both look. The crazy lady had stomped her foot and was giving them both a death glare while she drummed those fucking nails like she was trying to break the glass.

"Allie, are you going to take my order or not?"

Naw, forget this. Dax leaned on his elbows over the counter and gently put a hand over Pinkie's and pressed down until her fingers splayed out like candy-tipped spider legs and flattened beneath his palm. Her mouth made a perfect 'O', but she didn't pull back.

"Lady, it depends on if you're paying full price or not. She doesn't have time to make two batches, one for half the price."

The woman tipped her chin up and straightened her spine. Her breasts pushed out against the expensive-looking fabric of her pink button down. She was attractive for her age, Dax had to give her that. Considering how nicely she was groomed and the stylish clothes, she was used to being impeccable and, in her youth, probably drew a lot of male attention. She was also spoiled and used to getting her way.

"Fine," she ground out. "But I expect mine to be made first, Allie. Am I clear? Oh, and I'll need you to dress nicely and help serve at the event."

Dax smirked and pulled his hand away. She tipped her head in impatience, which only got worse when Allie didn't respond. Allie was staring unabashedly at him. Her beautiful eyes were wide and soft, her lips parted just enough that he could see a distinct line between them.

Pink flushed her cheeks and if he didn't know better, he'd think she was hung up on him right then.

"Yes," Allie finally said without looking away. Dax couldn't stop searching her eyes. His brow fell as he tried to sort the myriad emotions going across her face. The door jingled open and shut and he was aware someone had either come in or left, but he didn't care which.

His breathing hitched, his hands itching to grasp her face between them and pull her up for his kiss. Allie launched at him, stepping into his arms as she reached up, looped her hands around his neck and pulled him down, her lips crushing to his.

Mind whirling, he pushed his tongue between her lips and groaned as she parted for him. Her face angled so their mouths meshed, her kiss consuming him with her sweet, intoxicating taste. The bear inside him roared to life. It wanted more.

It wanted its mate.

Chapter Five

♥

"Well, I never!"

Marybeth's harsh voice sliced through the joy and pure lust clouding Allie's brain. With a start, she pulled back, confused over what she was doing. She had no control of that kiss, as if her body had taken over and was doing whatever the hell it wanted.

Every inch of her longed to be pressed against Dax, her lips on his, her hands wandering his spectacular body. "What are you doing to me?"

He looked every bit as confused as she felt. A pang of regret went through her as she stepped out of his arms and wiped her palms on her skirt to try and steady herself. Afraid to look at Marybeth or Dax, she quickly picked up the paper order book on the counter and cleared her throat.

She'd never felt this muddled in her life.

"Now, what... what exactly did you decide to order, Marybeth?"

A gentle touch on her wrist drew her attention. Her father sidled up next to her and took the order book, with a hushed, "I've got this," and a wink. Mortified that her father might have witnessed her wanton display—Becks too—Allie's cheeks went hot.

Wordlessly, she slipped into the back. She'd left a saucepan of boiled caramel frosting on the butcherblock to cool. Picking it up, she began to stir it, completely lost in what had just happened. Dax was attractive, yes. He was a woman's dream; yes. But she'd never acted so boldly, especially in front of a customer! His mouth had tasted so good, so familiar and satisfying as if she'd been waiting to experience him while already knowing how satisfying it would be.

The ache between her legs doubled in tenacity. Pressing her thighs together, Allie took a deep breath. What was wrong with her?

"You know, animals are purely attracted to each other by scent."

Dax stood at the end of the butcherblock counter, having arrived as silently as before. Allie didn't acknowledge him and kept stirring. She wanted to throw her arms around him again, but she steeled herself to her spot. And he damn well better stay put, too.

"The bear inside me is very attracted to how sweet you smell."

Her skin warmed under his gaze, the needy ache getting worse. Dax took a step closer, then another. Allie side-eyed him and stirred faster. She tried to measure her breathing, not too fast, not too slow.

"Sugar, cinnamon, chocolate... and my favorite, honey. It's like a perfume." His voice grew thick and low. "But you know which scent I love the most?"

Allie looked at him, holding the spoon in the air because she'd forgotten what she was doing. She didn't want to answer him, didn't want to encourage whatever this crazy thing was between them. But her lips moved anyway.

"What?"

His fingers grazed along her forearm. Allie jumped, her eyes closing against the electric sensations drawing over her skin. Lightly raking his nails along her arm, Dax stepped into her, tipping her chin up with his other hand so she met his eyes.

"The scent of your arousal. I know you want me, Allie. It's driving me and my bear wild."

How dare he imply... oh heck, he wasn't implying. It was fact. She did want him. Against better judgement and even with the likelihood this would turn into another heartbreak, or worse, she wanted him. Her mind was already cloudy again, as if this were happening by compulsion and not her own rational intentions.

Dax ran a hand around her ribs to her lower back and pulled her into him. She reached up, forgetting about the spoon in her hand. It stuck to the side of his neck, a big dollop of frosting coating his skin. It clung for a second, then ran in a slow, sensual glide over his neck where it settled in the crevice of his collarbone.

His eyebrows rose, his mouth pulling into a surprised grin. Allie gasped in apology but didn't move away to grab a rag. A better idea popped into her mind. She rose on her tiptoes until her lips almost touched his neck. Dax's chest swelled and stilled as her breath touched his skin.

"Now you're a sticky sweet bear." Allie touched the tip of her tongue to the frosting. Dax groaned, his fingers digging into her lower back. A surge of power and satisfaction rose in her chest. Moving closer, Allie slowly licked the side of his neck. The dual flavors of hot male skin and brown sugar was intoxicating. Her body was thrumming inside with a need that was going to quickly get out of control.

She had to slow this down. Leaning back a bit, she traced the divot in his chin with her finger. "See what I did there? Sticky Sweet, like the bakery..."

"Lick it off."

The dominance in his voice made her knees weak. His palm cupped the back of her head and directed her back to his neck. Allie leaned back in, stroking her tongue against his delicious skin with short and long strokes until she was trembling from head to toe. She sucked along the length of his neck and smoothed each pucker with a caress of her tongue.

Dax's breathing came hard and fast, a deeper sound of pleasure escaping from his lips. In one swift move, he grabbed her hips and spun her. He hitched her butt up onto the butcherblock and nudged her knees apart so he could fit between them. Dax slid the kerchief off her head and fisted the back of her hair, pulling her head back. Allie gasped and put her arms out behind her to steady herself on the counter as he forced her upper body to arch. Afraid she was going to fall; she squeezed her thighs around his hips to anchor herself.

Dax's pelvis pressed into the cradle of her thighs. The bulge of his erection pressed into her upper thigh as he leaned over her, his hand tightening in her hair. Almost giddy with excitement and tension, Allie whimpered with need. Her guess was right; his cock felt thick and long. If it was that yummy through his jeans, what would it be like free and bare in her hand?

His lips cruised over her jaw and down her neck. Allie moaned softly as his chest hovered over hers, so his muscles brushed the hard tips of her breasts. Moving lower, Dax nibbled and kissed his way along her collar bone. She was aware that her father or Becks could walk back here at any moment. She was more aware that she was making uncontrollable moans that sounded way too loud in her ears.

Dax ground his hips against her, bringing the length of his bulge against her pussy. Allie cried out and pushed into him, seeking the contact. Needing it like air. His big hands grabbed her hips and pulled her down, so her butt was on the edge of the countertop.

"What are you doing to me woman?" He growled the words before taking her mouth in a crushing kiss. Allie opened, taking his tongue, and pressed her lips as deeply as she could against his. Dax thrust his hips, rubbing all that hardness where she needed it the most. He pulled up her skirt with one hand and bunched it around her upper thighs. His eyes fell to the slip of her pink panties, the center soaked with her arousal.

"Fuck, you're wet." He pressed his cock against her again, expertly rubbing against her clit with a slow series of up and down thrusts. She tried to pull his shirt free from his jeans with one shaking hand but lost the strength. Captured in the pleasure pumping through her, she leaned back, her hair hanging down. Dax's warmth and scent and the pressure of his dominant hands on her body consumed her.

This was obscene, and sooooo improper and wrong.

But Jesus, the sweet pressure was already swelling between her legs, the erotic ride up, up, up to the peak of orgasm ushering her along. Trying to hush her moans, Allie knew she should plead with him to stop. But she didn't want to.

Desire darkened his expression and turned it wild and primal. Seeing how much he wanted her drove her that much closer to the edge. Pleasure thrummed around her clit. A familiar pressure started deep inside her pussy. The intensity of it left her breathless. She never came this fast! She was so overdue for an orgasm as it was, and this—this promised to be a doozy.

"Spread wider," he growled. Dax stroked her pussy lips with two long fingers, teasing her slit until she was desperate for him to go deeper. Allie let her thighs fall completely apart and he slipped between her lips. Electric pleasure sparked in every direction. She cried out, immediately aware of how loud she'd been and covered her mouth with her hand.

"No, no, don't be quiet. Let me hear how much you want me to make you cum."

The pressure deep within her pussy became demanding and powerful. She hadn't felt it in too long, this deep, deep ache that rolled into a demanding pulse she couldn't control or ignore. If Dax kept stroking her clit, she was going to explode in more ways than one.

"Wait!" She moaned and grabbed his wrist to stop his movements. Dax kissed her neck and kept fingering her clit. "I mean it, please."

He stalled. "Why?"

"B—because I can't come. Not here. We're in the *kitchen*!"

Dax drew back to look down at her. "Honey, your clit is so hard and swollen. You need to come."

She nodded even as an embarrassed flush heated her face. "Yes, God yes. But grab a towel or something."

His eyes narrowed before a decadent and wicked smile curved his mouth. His nostrils flared and for a second, Allie thought he might throw her over his shoulder and carry her off. Looking behind him, he spied a stack of folded kitchen towels and grabbed one. In a few seconds, he had it between her and the countertop.

Dax's fingers resumed a slow, torturous stroking. He slipped two fingers inside her and pressed gently upward against her pelvic bone. A bolt of blazing sensation raced through her. She tensed but quickly stopped trying to fight it. She was vaguely aware of sounds coming from the store, but she couldn't focus. The pleasure was off the charts amazing.

His lips grazed against her ear as his fingers began a gentle rocking motion while he kept pressure on that spot. That delicious, make-her-come-apart spot. Her entire body tensed as a huge pulse of pleasure rolled through her from the deepest place inside her pussy all the way to her clit. Allie grabbed his shoulders and came up off the counter.

"I'm going to cum!" The hurried words got lost in the moan she tried to silence. The orgasm hit her hard, yet she tensed her inner muscles to hold back. The pleasure refused to be denied and skyrocketed in sensation. She squirmed on the counter, gripping Dax as she thrust her hips into his hand, seeking every ounce of pleasure from his fingers. His fingers kept gently rocking until he'd milked her dry. Gasping, Allie slipped an arm around his neck to steady herself as the sensations began to fade like dying embers. Seconds passed with her heart racing and slamming in her chest. Dax gathered her into his arms as he leaned over her, holding her until their breathing slowed.

Reality came back in by degrees, her mind suddenly clearing with crystal clarity with what she'd just done.

In her bakery.

With a man she barely knew.

A quick glance at the clock revealed that he'd gotten her off in five minutes. Five fucking minutes!

"Oh, God," Allie burst. She wiggled against him until he stood back. He had a wadded up white towel in his hands and a very, very satisfied look on his face. She slipped off the counter and smoothed her skirt. Looking around, she was sure she'd find her dad standing there. But it was just her and Dax and the amazing ache of satiated lust, and the towel he'd used to remind her she'd let herself completely go in his arms.

He was looking at her with a heated want that she'd never seen on a man's face before. So much for taking it slow. She had to get this back on track before it turned into a complete disaster.

"You need to leave before someone sees us back here." She swallowed hard and crossed her arms over her breasts. Dax's gaze trailed to her chest. She couldn't help a glance at his erection still begging for release from his jeans. A pang went through her that she wouldn't get to feel that huge cock inside her right now or get him off. Poor guy. But they had to get back to boundaries... as if they had any to start with.

"Did you hear me? Slip out the back door so my dad thinks you already left."

He was still staring at her breasts. "Next time, those are going in my mouth."

Allie huffed a laugh and pushed him back another step so she could move to the side. "There isn't going to be a next time."

"Don't be so quick to say that."

She shook her head. "I won't rush into anything. I mean, I say that after we just... I know it makes me a hypocrite, but I can't rush again. I just can't."

"Allie, this isn't what you think it is." His forehead crinkled as if he'd just confused himself. Good, they could be confused together.

"Do I want to know what you mean by that?"

He ran a hand through his hair but looked as cocky as ever. Like he'd just learned a juicy secret.

"I want it all, Allie. I want you under me, on top of me, on your knees for me."

She opened her mouth to remind him there wouldn't be a next time, but he shushed her with a finger to her lips. She had the strongest urge to pull that finger into her mouth and give it a good suck.

"It feels like I have no control over this crazy attraction between us. It's like wanting you is the most natural thing."

So, he felt it, too. She searched his eyes and slowly nodded. Dax took her hand and gave it a gentle squeeze.

"If you feel it too, it can only mean one thing."

Allie put her hands up. "I don't want to hear it. I can't do this right now, okay? I've already been with a shifter who played the whole mate card, and he rejected me. It was a bad, scary relationship and I don't want this right now, ok? I don't want it."

Why was panic fluttering like a caged bird inside her? The room seemed small, suffocating. She couldn't do this, not now. Not again so soon. He was a shifter, just like Blake. Not all men were the same; she knew that deep down. On the surface, she was still scared of what Blake was capable of. He'd said things, done things she'd never told anyone about. Besides, she knew nothing about Dax except that she had some crazy strong attraction to him.

And it was confusing as hell. Relationships didn't happen this fast. It was supposed to take time before she had any important feelings for a man. And though she couldn't name exactly what she was feeling, it was something... *important.*

Dax's fingers curled into fists. "Which pack is he from?"

"What?"

All traces of lust were gone from his face. His eyes were hard, wicked. "The shifter who hurt you. Which pack, Allie?"

"Hey, Allie?" Her dad popped his head through the doors. "I need you out here."

She glanced down at herself to make sure her dress was back to normal. "Be right there."

"Allie." Dax lightly gripped her hand, but she pulled away.

"I have to go." She turned and hurried to the restroom. Closing the stall door, Allie leaned against it and closed her eyes.

She couldn't do it, not after so much heartbreak and so much longing for the one thing that never seemed to work out. All the years of her life she'd invested in men, both shifter and human, just hoping to find

The One, only to have it all go to waste? This is how the universe was going to play its hand, by throwing a man at her feet and deciding he was Mr. Right, right now? Screw that.

It didn't matter what he said, she wasn't getting involved with him. No matter what.

Chapter Six

♥

Dax gave another swing of the axe and welcomed the jarring discomfort that rippled up his arms and through his back. He needed the pain.

What he really needed was to shed his human skin, free his bear, and hunt in the forests of his father's land. His father had gone inside his massive log home, a perk of so many years of hard work and persistence in the uncertain construction industry. He'd looked a little ashen while operating the log splitter, and Dax was glad he'd gone to rest. At one-hundred twenty-five in human years, his dad was officially in a shifter's "golden years." It was hard to see his father as an old man, but that's what he was. And soon he'd be handing down Mitchell Corp to his sons, with Dax first in line. Unless of course, he made good on his promise to cut him out.

Dax pondered how easily his father had been tiring lately. He was slowing down; getting closer to the day he just couldn't keep up anymore. He's not been the same since mom died, Dax thought. In the three years since, his dad had been aging noticeably by increments, each year making it more obvious. No wonder he was so insistent that Dax take a mate. Rowan was growlingly aware of his mortality, and wanted things buttoned up as much as possible before he kicked the big one.

"Up for a challenge?"

Dax gave a sideways look to his younger brother Jett who pulled off his tee shirt and tossed it on the ground. He slung an axe to his shoulder and kicked over a few logs. Standing one upright on the extra chopping block, Jett wagged his eyebrows, waiting for Dax's response.

"Don't you have bees to sing to or something?"

Jett smiled his big, extra-white grin. You'd never know he was a beekeeper by looking at him. His beard was seriously overgrown, and he had the whole gruff mountain man thing going on. Hard to believe this guy played classical music to beehives that produced rainbow-colored honey.

"Nah, they're on a 90's rock kick and that's out of my range."

Jett nudged his log into place, stood back and squared his stance, then swung the axe down. The log split with a resounding crack and filled the air with the scent of fresh pine. Dax nodded to the pile he'd already chopped, nearly as high as he was tall.

"You must have something on your mind if you're splitting that much by hand." Jett inquired with an expectant look.

Dax was about to ignore the question in that sentence but turned it around instead. "I could say the same of you. There's a perfectly good hydraulic log splitter sitting right here that will save your back."

"My back doesn't need saving."

Jett picked up another log and split it in the blink of an eye. Dax didn't press. He didn't have to. Anyone close to Jett knew what caused his sudden and random depression and anxiety. It had been two years since Jett lost his mate and baby daughter in a freak accident, but to Jett, it probably felt like mere minutes.

First, they'd lost their mother and then Jett lost his family. Dax glanced back at the house. They couldn't lose Rowan, too. His father's insistence that he take a mate had been an aggravating thorn in his side for years now. Dax didn't know how to explain that he was holding out to find the kind of love his mom and dad had. In a romanticized way, he knew that real love like that existed.

He thought of Allie and his middle tightened up.

He wanted her. If she continued to reject him, he'd have to take a mate at the gathering. Maybe it was time to consider what his father had been requesting.

Take a mate. Any mate.

The thought of any other woman made his heart sink.

Jett had mostly quit the family business, helping out only here and there, putting even more pressure on Dax to step up. He'd bought a small farm on the outskirts of town, raised bees, and made crazy good things out of the honey. Dax jokingly called him Honey Bear, something Jett took to heart and used to name his brand of creations. His sales pitch was easy. Who didn't want to buy honey from an honest to goodness bear shifter?

Their younger brother, Desi, was a Marine and hadn't been home in years. They all kept hoping he'd wrap up soldier life and get his ass back to the pack. If Rowan continued to decline, Dax just may have to go get his baby brother himself and drag him home.

Jett ran a hand through his black hair. "You gonna race me or not?"

Jett split another log and kicked the pieces away. Well, his brother obviously had some demons to work out today, so who was Dax to deny him? With a sigh, he whipped off his own shirt which was already soaked clear through on the back. They each gathered logs and put one on their chopping blocks.

They raised their axes, and without an official start, began splitting the logs one after the other. kicking the split pieces off and putting a new one on. It was easy work, considering they were both pushing six-four and had bodies harboring the strong efficiency of a bear. Jett blew through his pile first and took his time gathering new logs.

"You're slowing down, big brother." Jett razzed.

"I'm going easy on you."

"Yeah, fuck you." Jett put two logs on the block and split them one after the other, his blade moving so fast, if you blinked, you'd miss it.

"Show off."

Dax went about the rest of his pile steadily, without the frenetic pace of his brother. Jett would wear himself out eventually, and if history were any indicator, Dax would need to make him stop before he literally collapsed in exhaustion.

"How'd that bourbon infused honey ever turn out?" Dax prompted as he eyed his brother to monitor his progress. Jett was sweating now, his massive chest and shoulders slick with a sheen.

"Man, it's so good. Tried some on toast today, and it was amazing. Would be even better on Frannie's apple cream cheese muffins..."

Dax's gut fell as his brother's voice trailed off and he kept swinging, dropping the topic. Just when he thought they'd find another rhythm in chopping, Jett turned to him and set the axe against his shoulder.

"Tell me about this woman."

Dax paused. "What woman?"

Jett scoffed. "The one I smell on you. Her scent is rolling off you like you took a bath with her."

Fuck, he wished. "I'm doing some work on her bakery, Sticky Sweet, where dad gets those rolls he loves."

Jett looked Dax up and down, the humor in his eyes saying he knew there was more to it.

"You don't smell like you've just been in the same room with her. It smells like you had your hand in her — "

Heat raced down Dax's spine and he straightened to his full height. "Watch yourself, Jett."

His brother's eyes narrowed at the implied threat in Dax's posture. A low rumble came from his throat, but his grin widened. "Good for you, big brother. I hope she's the one."

With that, Jett dropped the axe and bent to get his shirt. He wiped his face on the wadded-up material before slipping it back on. Dax wanted to talk about it, but he was hesitant to bring up anything about mates when his brother had lost his. Shifters only had one chance to take a mate, one chance to produce cubs. Jett had his, and now faced a life exactly as Rowan predicted Dax would: single, childless. Alone.

"Let me guess. She wants nothing to do with you."

Dax set his axe aside. "Sort of. How did you know?"

"Your face. You look like a love-struck cub."

"Yeah, well." Dax shrugged off the conversation. He didn't really want to talk about this after all. Jett ran a hand through his thick, black hair and pierced Dax with violet-blue eyes.

"You think she's your mate?"

Without a doubt. "Yes."

Jett spread his hands wide as if he didn't know what the problem was. "You're a fucking bear, Dax. Deep down, you know how to get her to cooperate. What do male shifters resort to when their women are being stubborn?"

Dax shook his head. "That only works on shifter females. This one is human. She'll kill me."

Jett rolled his eyes and walked past him toward the house.

"Guess you'll be one lonely son of a bitch like me, then."

Dax softened at his brother's words but doubt just multiplied. He couldn't just... he'd never heard of a shifter doing that to a human woman. He couldn't.

Could he?

Chapter Seven

♥

Allie drowned her guilt with a second glass of wine.

Her dad was on a "date" with Marybeth right now because of her little make out session with Dax. Every time she thought about it, Allie wanted to kick herself for being so dumb! Marybeth had made it very clear that Ben had to accompany her to dinner tonight if Allie wanted to keep her massive bakery order or she was giving it to Bella Blu.

The order she'd made bigger by adding fifty cherry almond pastries. Christ, MB, and her blackmail.

It was getting late. She and Becks had spent the day fixing the last of the superficial raccoon damage, and aside from the claw marks in the wall, chewed up trim and the broken ceiling, the store was looking back to normal. Dax had sent her a text that he'd bring her a quote on the repair costs soon. She was ready to get back on schedule and open her damn store. Trying to ignore what she and Dax had done, she sterilized the entire kitchen and all its contents, getting it ready to produce baked goods for sale.

Allie laid each recipe out on the counter and started writing an ingredients list. Nothing could be made too far ahead of time, but she could get all the prep work done so the baking could begin two nights before Marybeth's party. She'd have to bring one of her staff back, including Becks, and probably her dad, too, to get done in time.

Especially if Dax had been serious about his order.

She huffed a laugh. His order had been a tactic to get under Marybeth's skin, that's all. The way he stepped up for her was both impressive and annoying. She didn't need him standing up for her, but on the other hand, it was kind of nice. Dax wasn't the kind to take shit from anyone, she could tell. She was very attracted to that. The dominance, the...what would you call it? Alpha attitude? Sure, he was cocky, but the primal female in her was satisfied with his dominate nature. She'd be protected by him, cared for.

The feeling of security she had when she was around him was refreshing, and not something she knew she needed until now.

Allie tried to focus on her list, but her mind was other places. Dax.

Dax.

Dax.

Damn, Dax.

With a sigh, she resolved to not bother going home tonight. It was only seven p.m., and she wasn't a lick tired. Her cell phone buzzed. Pulling it from her pocket, Allie hesitated before checking the screen. She suspected it would be Blake before she even looked.

I've had enough of your silence, Allie.

Her brow knitted as a blip of fear bubbled inside her chest. Was that a threat? She hadn't responded to any of his past messages. She didn't owe him a damn thing! Their breakup hadn't been exactly clean. After he'd publicly humiliated her, he'd done a one-eighty and begged for her to come back to him. He'd texted and called repeatedly for weeks afterward and drove past her house at random times. Then he'd moved, and the harassment had stopped just as she was considering a restraining order, of course.

Tightening her jaw, Allie responded. *Leave me alone, Blake. I'm not interested in speaking to you.*

She watched the screen, knowing Blake well enough to figure he'd have an immediate response to her rejection. A minute or two passed with nothing. Glad that she was wrong in her assumption, she moved to put the cell in her back pocket when a loud knock came from the front door.

She froze. She had a single light on behind the counter as she always did at night, and the front shades pulled down. Blake wouldn't... would he?

"Allie? It's me. I'm coming in."

She let out a breath at Dax's voice.

The door opened, and he stepped inside. He moved effortlessly, with a kind of manly grace that made it hard to look away. His body was in perfect coordination, the sleek muscles and supple skin definitively masculine. He held a paper bag in the crook of one arm. It crinkled as he made a half turn to close the door, and heaven help her, his jeans fit him perfectly!

"Didn't want to scare you by just coming in." His eyes narrowed, and his face carried a tension she'd never seen on him before. "You do look scared. I'm sorry."

Allie waved him off. "It's nothing. What are you doing here?"

The tension she'd been carrying in her shoulders all day melted away as she drank in the sight of him. Honestly, she'd been like a teenager with a hard crush trying to stay busy to keep her mind from wondering when she'd see him again. Having a lot to do hadn't worked in keeping the nervous energy at bay.

Now a different kind of tension replaced it. Allie grew warm between her thighs, with an ache that was becoming a familiar byproduct of Dax's presence.

His blonde hair was wavy and tousled, as if he'd been running his long, sculpted fingers through it often.

"Saw the back lights on. Thought I'd stop by."

He carried himself like he was expecting a blow at any moment. His upper body appeared tense, and he stood completely straight which made his impressive height and build even more intimidating.

And delicious.

"Okay." Allie smiled faintly. "But, why?"

What was wrong with him? He was staring at her like he was about to devour her or do something illegal. Maybe both. Now that she thought about it, he did have an air of nervousness about him that seemed out of place. He was normally so cocky and sure of himself.

"Is everything okay?" She asked carefully.

Despite her relationship with one, she didn't know much about shifters. Maybe he'd just been in his animal form and was transitioning back into his human state of mind. A shudder went through her at the thought. She'd love to see him morph into his bear. All that power and strength and wildness. He was deadly, but he was also gentle. The two traits together were almost more than her ovaries could handle.

His gaze bore into her so intently, Allie had the urge to step back. But she didn't. He'd never given her a reason to believe he would be dangerous toward her. Just yesterday, he had her half naked on the counter while he gave her an orgasm. She'd been completely vulnerable to him and lived to tell the tale. If he'd meant her harm, she'd know it by now.

He wasn't Blake. She had to remind herself of that.

"Everything's fine."

Allie wasn't sure how much more tension she could take. Her entire body was getting warmer and the pulsing ache between her legs was a hundred times worse. He'd mentioned before that he could smell her arousal.

She was probably saturating him with it now. How did he affect her like this?

Allie fidgeted with a pencil and looked at her list to try and center herself.

"Well, I have a lot to do tonight, so is there something I can help you with, or...?"

If he was going to stand there and be slightly creepy, and amazingly hot, while staring at her, he could get out. She really did have stuff to do. And thanks to him, she was going to have a hard time keeping her head on her work and not thinking about his dick and how mouth-watering he looked in that blue tee shirt.

Dax shoved his hands in his front pockets, another move that surprised her. He liked to use his hands for expression when he spoke. She didn't peg him as the more submissive, hands-in-pockets type. She hitched an eyebrow. Maybe he was trying to keep from touching her.

"You have plans for tonight."

What was wrong with him? His expression had a predatory shadow to it, which made her wonder again if he'd recently shifted.

"No... not aside from getting started on your chocolate cupcakes. You really wanted those, right?"

"It wasn't a question. I'm telling you that you have plans tonight."

Allie put her pencil down, trying to feel out that statement. Why did she feel so excited? Frustrated by the mixed signals, she picked up her list. He could stand there looking all angsty and tortured if he wanted to. She had a pot of coffee to brew and start drinking if she was going to pull an all-nighter.

"I appreciate the caveman thing you have going on right now, but you can show yourself out."

Dax looked slightly amused. "Caveman thing?"

"Yeah," Allie said as she reached for her apron and tied it on. "I feel like you're going to throw me over your shoulder and carry me off somewhere."

"You could tell?"

She did a double take at him, confounded. "What do you mean, I could tell?"

Whatever fog had been hanging over him faded off, leaving behind the playful and self-assured man she was getting accustomed to. He sauntered over and put the bag on the counter.

"I *was* going to carry you off. Over my shoulder and everything."

Allie started to laugh, but he looked completely serious. Dax shrugged and pulled a bottle of wine from the bag. "It's how shifter men get a woman they're interested in to come around."

"That's barbaric. And illegal. And completely sexist." Allie threw up her hands. "What if the woman isn't interested in you? You carry her off and hope she'll change her mind?"

"No. It only works when a shifter knows the woman is interested, but for whatever reason, is being a difficult shrew."

"You're calling me a shrew?"

"It's a reference."

"A really insulting one."

"Kind of like calling me a caveman?"

She huffed and grabbed her signature coffee cup off the stainless-steel table by the door. Dax came through the service door and took the mug, grabbed her hand, and pulled her into him. Allie gasped but didn't resist. Her body started to sing at the press of his hard torso against her soft, hard-peaked breasts. He set the mug down with the wordage facing them.

"Yeah, yeah, the tears of your enemies. I know. But I'm not your enemy, Allie. You can have my tears. You can have my blood, my body. My heart. All of it. You could easily take whatever you wanted from me, and I wouldn't be able to stop it—I wouldn't *want* to stop it—because you're my mate."

She tried to ignore the joyous emotion welling up inside her, as if her very soul was screaming, "yes, yes, yes!" to his theory. But it was absurd. People didn't do this. This isn't how love is supposed to go. History showed her what happened when she rushed. No more rushing love!

Besides, what if it wasn't true and real? What if he changed his mind, just like Blake had?

"No, I'm not."

Even as she spoke the words, Allie knew they were wrong. Resisting made the truth less glaring, though. She didn't want it to go like this. After months and years of waiting and hoping for the right guy to show up, well, she wanted the slow, sweet, and steady fall. Being blindsided by a man she'd only known a few days wasn't at all what she was expecting.

How could she trust the little voice inside that said he was the man for her?

Dax's eyes drew down her body, making her flush. He paused at her waist where the tie to her apron had come loose. His fingers trailed slowly over her sides, fleshing out a reminder of how it had felt to be under his hands while he made her cum. Little electric sparks jumped on her heated skin. He trailed along the tie and pulled the loose knot free with one finger.

Allie let out a breath. His head was bent as he worked to slowly work the strings, all that golden hair at the perfect level for her to dig her fingers into. She itched to do just that, but held back, too consumed by the sweet sensation of his fingers brushing against her body.

"One thing about bear shifters, Allie." Dax said in a low voice. "Is that we can sense the key element in a female that makes them compatible as a mate."

His palms gripped her hips, his fingers splaying wide over the rise of her ass. She moaned and closed her eyes as his face moved to the crook of her neck. His breath washed over the exposed skin there, his lips promising a kiss there.

God, how she wanted him to.

"Do you know what the key element is?"

She shook her head, too enraptured to speak. She might be suspicious in how fast she'd become attracted to him, but she couldn't deny the immediate and forceful pull he had over her body.

Dax's lips feathered over the curve in her neck. Allie jerked at the gentle touch, her fingers knotting into fists to keep from pulling him closer. Yet, her head fell to the side in complete supplication. It might be wrong to take the pleasure he was offering her, but she didn't care.

She'd be a selfish bitch, just this once. Because damn, she'd never felt like this before.

"Your scent is the key. Usually, only the man meant to be your mate can detect it. Sometimes more than one can, and then you get the classic love war. But your scent, Allie. It's just for me."

One big, warm hand pressed into her lower back. He gripped the hair at the back of her head with the other. In one gentle but firm move, he pulled her head back and hovered his lips over hers.

"You weren't truly compatible with the shifter you dated."

She made a noise of disgust. "Thankfully."

Dax brushed her lips with his. "Was he an Alpha?"

She wanted to sink into the sensations roving her body, but she gave herself a mental slap.

"I... I don't know the difference."

Dax cruised her jaw with his lips. "I'm an Alpha. Our genetics are strong, demanding, and potent. We must take mates and produce cubs before our thirty-fourth birthday, or we lose the ability. Beta shifters get a little longer. Drone shifters are the lowest, the weakest. They can mate their entire lives, because their genetics are weak, and it often takes several tries for them to successfully reproduce."

He kissed her neck with luxurious slowness. Her mind absorbed his words, but she didn't really process them.

"He... wasn't an Alpha."

Dax groaned—or was that a growl?

"A woman like you demands an Alpha. You're mine, Allie. Deep down, you already know that, don't you?"

She breathed against his mouth, her body tight with anticipation. She felt equal parts safe and nervous, and with everything inside her, she loved his dominance. No man had ever taken control like this. She didn't even need to think about whether she liked it; it was instinctual and right now, she'd allow him to do anything he wanted. Allie gripped his sides, trying to hold him back while wanting nothing more than to pull him closer.

"Humans detect their most compatible partner initially by scent, too, but most are too far removed from their animalistic pasts to be conscious about it. The second component is taste." His lips brushed over hers. Allie parted her lips, immediately seeking more.

Dax grinned. "I already know you taste amazing, and I want more."

His mouth covered hers in a deep draw that meshed their tongues and breath. The kiss pulled the plug on her restraint. Allie wrapped her arms around him, pulling him closer with a desperation she'd never experienced before. Her flesh ached to feel him hot and naked along every inch of her body. She wanted his lips and hands all over her, his cock filling her until she was completely dominated by him.

She worked her left leg around his thigh and hitched it as high as she could. Pressing her hips into him, Allie grabbed fistfuls of his shirt.

Dax smiled against her mouth. Allie realized what she was doing. She was literally trying to climb him.

"See? Look what a wild kitten you are for me."

Disgusted with her lack of restraint, Allie put her palms on Dax's chest, and with a pang of regret, pushed him back. He moved but kept one hand on her hip.

"This is getting out of hand," Allie breathed. What an understatement. That's twice now she'd almost had sex with Dax in her bakery, of all places. Despite the shame in that, she wanted him to pull her right back against his body and pick up where they left off.

But this had to stop. She wasn't after the one-night fling, and really, how could this be more than that? All this talk about her being his mate was nothing more than a bad shifter pick-up line.

She crossed her arms. "You should go. I have a lot to do."

"Why do you keep resisting what's happening so naturally between us?" He gently squeezed her hip in a kneading motion that sent shivers down her spine. Her body's response made it difficult to refute his statement.

She couldn't bring herself to answer because thoughtful words refused to come. After a moment, he gave a slight nod as if acquiescing to her hesitation in continuing the conversation. He spread his hands wide.

"Make me your servant. How can I help?"

She hitched an eyebrow. A sudden image of Dax in a pink apron and nothing else, with a mixing bowl in the crook of one elbow came to mind. She could refuse his help, but though she was trying to keep space between them to slow down this crazy heat, she didn't really want him to go. Her usually chaotic mind seemed more at peace when he was around. If he wrapped her up in his arms and held her through the night, she'd probably sleep for hours straight. He had a calming effect on her that she was coming to crave.

A random idea popped into her head.

"Were you serious about ordering the chocolate bacon cupcakes?"

"Hell yes. My family is having a... party of sorts and I think they'd be a hit."

Allie nodded that he should follow her as she walked into the back and went to the refrigerator.

"I imagine it takes a lot of food to feed a party of bear shifters. Let's make that test batch you mentioned."

She grabbed out some heavy cream, butter, and eggs and made a half turn to deposit them into Dax's waiting hands. He was looking at her ass and not even trying to hide it. She plopped a small package of bacon onto his pile. He followed her obediently across the room as she took down flour, baking chocolate and vanilla. She reached for a stainless-steel bowl below the worktable at Dax's hip. He didn't move, forcing her to brush against his thigh to grab it. She stood and gave him an annoyed look—one that deepened as his gaze fell to her breasts.

"We have big appetites; that's true."

She set the bowl down hard. "Focus, man."

He put his hands up in mock surrender. Allie giggled. Warm contentment spread through her, and she had to swallow hard to keep herself focused.

Dax proved a willing helper as she instructed him on how to make the cupcake batter. He melted chocolate without burning it, only drank half the stout ale and somehow managed to refrain from eating all the bacon. By the time the cupcakes were in the oven, his face was streaked with flour and his shirt had come untucked.

"Frosting time," she prompted. She'd already melted more chocolate and it sat like a decadent pool in the bottom of the waiting bowl. "Here, add in this powdered sugar."

Dax took the measuring cup of fluffy sugar and, before she could stop him, dumped it in all at once. The powder billowed up like a cloud and spilled all over the counter. Coughing, Allie waved in front of her face as he did the same. They looked at each other and she couldn't hold back laughter. His gorgeous face was covered in shimmery, white dust.

He wiped his face with one hand. "That's not regular sugar."

Allie laughed as she swept his bottom lip with her thumb. "No, but it's still sweet."

Impulsively, she brushed her thumb over his sugar-coated lips. The humor between them died as lust quickly replaced it. Damn, why had she done that? Unable to help herself, she popped her finger between her lips and sucked the confection off.

Why did he taste so good? She licked her lips again savoring the faint taste of his lips blended with the added sweetness.

Dax's face grew dark, his expression a twin to the one he wore when he'd first walked in tonight.

"Damn it, Allie."

A hard breath squeezed out of her, and she knew there was no way to stop the passion between them. The timer on the oven beeped, pulling her attention away from the man with the serious sex face. Glad for the distraction, she turned off the oven and opened the door to pull the test batch of cupcakes out. She set them on the counter and was about to slip off the oven mitt when Dax's arm went around her waist from behind. He spun her so her breasts bumped into his chest right before he hauled her up and over his shoulder.

Just like he'd threatened to do.

She gasped and flailed to grab ahold of something for support. Twisting a little, she tried to shimmy down, but his grip was too serious, too strong.

"Dax!"

This couldn't be happening. This... this was insane! Men didn't just carry women off over their shoulders and whisk them away like this. Dax was oblivious to manners and the law, obviously.

"You can't really do this!"

He strode through the kitchen as if she weighed nothing. She was a little dizzy from being mostly upside down by the time he got to the front door. Locking the door, he turned off the lights save for the one soft glow she kept on behind the counter.

"Then why'd you stop struggling?"

Had she? Allie gripped big handfuls of the back of his tee shirt to keep herself steady. Her body was still.

"Because...I didn't want to fall while you — "

"Bullshit."

"Dax!"

He strode into the back of the bakery again, flipping off lights while she clung to him. "If you wanted down so badly, you'd be fighting me tooth and nail until I either dropped you or you wiggled free. Truth is, kitten, you don't want to be set down."

His palm came down hard on her ass. Allie's head shot up as a slight sting spread over her rear and punched a shot of pleasure between legs. Had he really just spanked her?

"You want me to take you home and fuck you until you're walking sideways. Don't you?"

She twisted, and the bulge of his shoulder dug into her belly. Every inch of her longed for more contact with his body, to feel his hands and lips on her skin. God, he was right! She wanted exactly what he'd said.

Dax saw her purse sitting on the end table in the back hall, grabbed it, and opened the back door. He stepped into the darkness outside, locked the door behind him and pulled it shut.

"Tell me you want this." His voice was so thick and low, she almost didn't hear him.

She took a breath. Let it out. Took another. Where was the anger? Why the hell wasn't she furious right now?

"I... I... yes. Okay? Yes."

His big palm cupped her ass right before he gave her another smack that forced a dart of pleasure between her legs.

"Fuck, woman, you're in for a hell of a night."

Chapter Eight

He'd never been this ready to give a woman pleasure in his life.

He'd had one-night stands, yes. But he'd never acted on the time old tradition of shifter men to simply carry off a female he wanted to make his mate. The rules said he had to keep her and mate her for three days and nights before she'd be officially his. Maybe the theory was that if he fucked her enough, she'd have no choice but to fall in love with him and agree to be his. Or maybe she'd be too exhausted afterward to protest.

He didn't care.

He wanted Allie and if the docile way she was sitting in his car was an indication, she wanted it too.

He hadn't really meant to be a caveman, but once Jett had put the idea in his head earlier, it was all Dax could think about. Then the instinct kicked in and he couldn't help himself. If she'd said no, he would have put her down and walked away. If she'd run away from him and called the cops and put him in jail for the night, it would have been her right and he would accept the consequences for being so bold.

But she'd said yes.

And the way she was looking at him right now still said yes.

The key sat in the ignition, waiting for the turn of his hand. His heart beat a nervous staccato inside his chest. It wasn't like him to feel this way. Nervousness and uncertainty were not in his repertoire, but the weight of importance on this one decision couldn't be denied.

Allie sat softly in the dark beside him, the glow of the streetlamps casting shadows around her pretty face. Her eyes were brilliant relief against the dim backdrop as she stared at him. Just looking at her made his body ache.

"My place is just outside of town, ten minutes from here."

"Allie — "

"Look," she grinned. "The answer is yes. And for the record, I like the caveman thing you had going on."

Dax started the truck and the roar of his Chevy had never been more musical. She moved as if she were going to pull her seatbelt on, but he stopped her with a tug on her wrist. She tilted sideways and half-twisted into him. Dax cupped her face with one hand, the other sliding around her body to hold her tight. She wanted caveman; she was going to get it.

Without mercy, he ground his lips into hers. His tongue demanded entrance between her plump lips. A groan pushed out of him as her slick heat welcomed the intrusion. God, how he couldn't wait to do that to her pussy. She cupped his face between her hands and pulled him closer, meeting his kiss with abandon.

Her breasts pushed against his forearm. He snaked a hand to the front of her shirt and quickly popped the top three buttons. Allie arched into him as he slid his hand inside the fabric and cupped her full, hard-tipped breast. He loved the soft weight in his hand and with an impatient tug, ripped the remaining buttons and cupped her other breast with his free hand. She gasped as his thumbs brushed over her nipples.

They had to get out of here before he positioned her curvy body under him, and they got tangled up in the front of his truck. Reluctantly, Dax pulled away and squared himself in the seat. Allie did the same, attempting to right her shirt before putting her seatbelt on with trembling hands. He could barely keep his eyes off her and on the road as he pulled away. Her breasts were mostly bare, thanks to the ripped shirt and askew bra. He should have ripped that away, too.

Allie gave him directions and somehow, he processed them. He'd taken a right, then a left and was about to speed up when she tucked the shoulder strap of her seatbelt under her arm and leaned over the center console. He glanced down as she began working the button of his jeans.

His heart skipped a beat as she pulled the zipper down and quickly opened his jeans.

"Allie."

Like he was going to stop her. No, he wanted whatever the hell she was about to do. She didn't respond. Her eyes were riveted to his crotch. Talk about an ego boost. Caressing him over his briefs, Allie worked the band of his underwear down and moaned as she bared the tip of his cock.

"Oh, yes," she gushed with appreciation. Her thumb swept the top and a little spiral of heat followed the movement of her finger. Dax groaned and slid down just a bit, silently begging in his mind for her to take him into her mouth.

She was beautiful, sexy, sassy, and a mind reader. Her breasts pressed into his thigh as her lips wrapped around his dick. Her mouth closed around him, sucking in a long, deep draw. His hips thrust forward, one hand leaving the steering wheel to cup the back of her head.

"God, suck me, Allie."

She pulled the waist of his underwear down as far as they would go, her mouth following down, down, down, taking him as much as she could. Her mouth stretched beneath his size as he hit the back of her throat. She made a small sound, her hand working his base as she mouthed him.

She pulled back and pumped him with her hand for a second. She stared at his cock with unmasked appreciation and his heart soared.

"Just think, that's going to be fucking your pussy real soon."

She smiled before diving back in, taking him into her mouth and riding him with a mix of aggression and softness. His balls tightened. He'd been dreaming of this so much that his body was primed for the release only she could bring.

His vision blurred, and he had to give himself a mental shake to keep steady on the road. Putting both hands back on the wheel, Dax was fighting the pleasure when something darted out into the road. He pressed the break, slowing fast but evenly. He grabbed onto Allie to keep her in place, but her head had already snapped up.

"Raccoon!" Dax said, coming to a near stop as the animal waddled across the road.

"Of course," Allie chuckled, ready to resume the position but he stopped her with a gentle tug on her hair.

"Better let me focus."

"No problem. We're here." She pointed to a cute little brick house at the end of the street. The Rocky Mountains cast an impressive shadowy backdrop. Grabbing her purse, she nearly bolted out of the truck. Dax followed, zipping up enough to be decent but not cause his raging erection any harm. They darted up her porch, hand in hand. Allie punched a number into the keypad to unlock the house. A single light shone from the living room as they walked in, casting a soft golden glow around the room.

He took Allie by the shoulders and pulled her into him, taking her mouth with his in a desperate, hard kiss. Her fingers threaded into his hair as he walked her over the hardwood floor to the couch. Her legs hit the cushion and Dax gave her a gentle shove.

Allie fell back onto the couch with a giggle, her breasts bouncing and her hair spreading all over the cushion. Dax put one of her legs high on the back of the couch and spread the other wide, kneeling between her legs as he hiked her skirt to her waist. Her sounds deepened from amusement to passion as he pulled her panties to the side. The heady perfume of her scent drew him like a bee to honey. Gently, he used two fingers to part her pussy lips and dipped his head between her thighs. Her clit was already swollen, her slit glistening with arousal and it took all his will not to drive his cock into her right then.

Dax flicked the tip of his tongue over her clit. Allie arched in surprise, her legs falling open wider at the simple touch. Restraint wasn't working well with him right now, so he gave up. There was a time to go slow, to savor. This wasn't it. He gripped her hips and pulled her down to his mouth. Without mercy, he stroked her clit with his tongue until she moaned and cried out and gripped his head like a lifeline. Her nub swelled beneath his mouth, her moans becoming more desperate.

"Dax, please!" Allie threw her head back and clamped her thighs around his face. Placing the heel of his hand on her pubic bone, he slid two fingers inside. Her ass came up off the bed as he found the spot just inside her pussy that set her off the last time. Bless the G-spot! She pushed against his hand with a desperate cry as he rocked his fingers with a back-and-forth motion.

Her inner muscles tightened, and she cried out his name. His cock ached with pleasure-pain and a need so strong, he had to give in. She was about to come, and he needed to feel her do it around his cock. Still working her pussy, he used his free hand to open his already loosened zipper, then wriggled his jeans down as far as he could.

"Yes, yes!" Allie watched him, her hands making a "come here" motion when she saw him kicking off his pants. He sucked her clit between his lips in one final tease, then slowly moved up her body. Her bra tangled beneath her breasts, freeing them. Dax took one rigid, pink nipple in his mouth as he urged her legs even farther apart with his knee.

Her hot heat welcomed the tip of his cock as he pressed and held against her softness.

"Now, please, now!" Allie cried out. She grabbed his hip with one hand and tilted her pelvis upward. Dax thrust, tempering himself to let her adjust to his size. But Allie wouldn't have it. She jerked her hips up, urging him inside with a frenzied passion. He didn't want to hurt her, but he wasn't going to deny her either.

He thrust deep. Their voices mixed as they cried out together. Her body stretched and tensed beneath him, her nipples grazing against his tee shirt. Allie grasped at the shirt, tugging, and pulling until he whipped it off with one hand and pressed his bare chest against her breasts. The skin-on-skin contact caused goosebumps to race over his flesh. Dax slowly withdrew and ran a palm lightly over her breast. With a hard thrust, he rubbed her nipple between his fingers and took her mouth in a deep kiss.

Allie panted as she met him thrust for thrust. Her slick pussy clamped down around his cock and the sensations were so intense, a slow tremor took over his body. He gathered Allie to him, lifting her hips as he drove into her. His length rubbed against the spot deep inside her; he felt it swell as her moans became more desperate. Dax felt barely in control of himself, as if this intimacy was out of his hands and he was completely at the will of his body.

"Dax!" Allie cried, gripping his shoulders, and grinding her pelvis against his. Suddenly, her inner muscles clamped down hard around his cock as she came.

"Oh, yeah," he groaned, riding her harder as his own climax began to unfurl.

She soaked him, her pussy tighter and slicker than ever. He felt outside of himself, with such thin control that he was about to lose it. His cock swelled, and his balls went tight as pleasure spiraled and begged to be set free. Dax tipped his head to the crook of Allie's neck, biting her gently there as his orgasm reached its peak.

Suddenly remembering this wasn't the Pairing, he withdrew and took his cock in his hand. Allie's brow furrowed as a desperate sound of protest escaped her lips. Her eyes were heavy-lidded as she watched him pump his cock. He thrust his hips so his tip sat just above her soft belly.

"Give it to me, Dax."

The soft but firm demand sent him over. Dax clenched his jaw as he came all over the soft rise of her belly. He gasped for breath as pleasure soaked him, a spiral of blackness taking over all rational thought until he was simultaneously aware that the epic sensations had waned, and he was half lying on top of Allie with his knees on the floor.

Her fingers were loose in his hair, a soft smile on her lips as she dozed. He could only look at her, taking in the angelic beauty of her sleeping face and struggled with how much his heart filled.

How full he felt inside.

How right.

Gently picking her up, Dax cradled her against his chest as he found his way to her room and set her on the bed. She moaned softly in a barely awake way as he stripped her bare, and then himself, before crawling beneath the covers next to her. Taking her into his arms, the full, satiated sensation inside him bloomed even more as she snuggled against him and thread her fingers into his.

If this is what his parents had together—even an ounce—he was glad he'd waited for it.

What was life without this?

It was nothing he could ever go back to.

# # #

Dax didn't want to wake her, but he recalled she'd mentioned meeting Becks at four-thirty this morning to start working and it was already well past that.

Her unruly curls splayed across the pillow. He threaded his fingers through them, gently separating the strands as he studied her soft expression. The big, full feeling came back in his chest. It was warm and heady, and he didn't want it to go away.

Talk about cutting it close. The moon would be full in three days' time. He had until then to convince her to become his mate or lose his chance forever. The warmth inside him began to shrivel at the idea she'd deny him. To lose her now, when he was completely sure she was meant for him—that they were meant for each other—was more than he could bear.

He couldn't give this up now. Not ever.

"Allie," he whispered while giving her a gentle shake.

She stirred, her brow furrowing in confusion, but a sleepy smile replaced it. She reached for him, and their fingers entwined before she flipped onto her back and rubbed her face.

"I don't want to get up."

The sheet fell midway, revealing her luscious, full breasts and the feminine flare of her ribs. He couldn't stop himself from touching her. With one finger, he trailed along the rise of her breast, stopping at the beautiful pink peak to tease and swirl, before continuing down...

"Keep that up and no one will be getting treats but me today." She swatted at his hand, but it was a half-ass attempt.

"No one but us," Dax replied. He covered her with his body, gently grinding the length of his erection into the soft V at her thighs. She didn't hesitate, just opened those perfect legs to allow him to settle between them. Damn sheet was between them, but it didn't deter the heat radiating off her. He closed his eyes as he ripped the sheet away and sank deeply into her.

His name dripped like the sweetest honey off her lips. Something in her tone made his heart soar with, what, hope? Her lips parted as if she had more to say, and he hoped she would.

Her cell phone rang.

They both jumped at the unexpected sound.

"Jesus," Allie groaned. She scrambled to reach her cell from the bedside table. Dax figured he could move, but he was enjoying the feel of her curvy body beneath his too much to let her go.

"Hello?" She answered before the phone was even to her ear. Dax didn't need to adjust his heightened senses to hear the woman on the other end. It was Becks.

"Hey, babe. You, uh, coming in soon?"

Allie gently pushed Dax off her and he relented with a ton of regret. She sat.

"On my way in ten. What's up?"

There was a pause. Allie's face scrunched, her shoulders going tense. "Becks?"

"There's someone here to see you."

The clock flashed 5:45 a.m., Becks' voice was tight and tense, and though he didn't know her well, it wasn't her normal. Allie seemed to think so too as she swung her feet over the side of the bed.

"Are you okay? Should I call the police?" She slid off the bed, leaving the sheet behind. Dax followed suit as Allie got dressed.

"I'm fine. Just... hurry."

Chapter Nine

The satisfying after-glow of having sex with Dax didn't wear off as she racked her brain to figure out who the hell would be at the bakery this time of morning.

Dax held her hand on the short drive to Sticky Sweet. It was a sweet gesture but seemed so natural and easy, as if they'd held hands a million times before. She couldn't stop sneaking peeks at him in the budding daylight. Everything between them seemed easy. From the first moment he'd walked into the bakery, she'd felt a comfort and familiarity she'd never experienced with a guy before. It was as if they'd simply fallen into place beside each other.

She squeezed her legs together, welcoming the soreness that would serve as an all-day reminder of the biggest pleasure she'd ever known. It was going to be damn difficult to think of anything else today.

Dax pulled into the front of the bakery. The street out front was empty of vehicles. Becks must have walked this morning since her bicycle wasn't parked in the rack. And the mystery visitor must have parked in the back. She didn't like it. The only good reason to park in the back lot this time of day was to avoid being seen from the main road. A quick look at Dax made it clear he was thinking the same thing.

An uneasy feeling went through her. Dax flexed his fingers and quivered a little as if he was suddenly uncomfortable in his own skin. Maybe the bear inside him was uneasy, too. Could it pick up on her feelings and emotions?

He went to Allie's door and opened it. Putting a hand on her wrist, he stopped her when she would have walked ahead.

"I'm going with you."

She felt a moment of protest but grabbed his hand in acceptance instead. "Okay."

Dax gave her a comforting sense of protection. The situation was odd, and she wasn't going to turn away a six-foot four shifter's offer to tag along in case something went south. She took out the key to the front door but found it already open.

Dax walked in first. "Becks?"

Allie pulled back with a start. A shadowy figure unfurled from the corner by the coffee bar. It took her brain a second to realize it was a man. Dax was already in motion, stepping in front of Allie with his big body taking up as much space as possible. In that nanosecond, recognition hit her, and she ducked around Dax to get a second look.

She did a double take. "Blake?"

A big smile cut across his narrow face as if this was a perfectly expected reunion at five something in the morning. An uncontrollable quiver took over her body. She hadn't seen him in months since he'd left the law firm in town for his home pack in Bentleyville. Though his text messages had bothered her, she'd felt safe in that he was long gone from Estes Park.

Not anymore.

"Hello, Allie."

Blake gave Dax a cursory glance, then ignored him to focus his attention on her. Dax stood partially in front of her, a protective move that she welcomed. His body was a shield, and she couldn't shake the sensation that she needed the protection.

Becks called out from behind the bakery case. "He told me I couldn't tell you he was here or he'd..."

Blake gave a half turn to glare at Becks. "Thank you, Becks. I'm sure you have things to do in the back."

"Don't speak to her like that. It's fine, Becks."

Having Dax so close gave Allie a sense of confidence. He was taller than Blake, and though they were both bear shifters, there was no denying Dax was bigger, stronger. She'd never seen either man shift into their bear, but she suspected there'd be no real competition between them there, either. Allie was still frustrated that she hadn't seen through her ex sooner. He was a terrible person.

He was the reason she'd started the Loser Allie List.

He was the reason she had to get cozy with a vibrator again.

He was the reason she'd been afraid of men for the first time in her life.

A low rumble came from behind her. Dax... did he just growl? He stood with his arms crossed and his feet spread wide. The two men mirrored each other, and with each second, Blake seemed to get more irritated.

"What are you doing here, Blake?"

In the arrogant way he had, Blake broke away from his stare down with Dax and started to wander around the store. He made a half circle around the room, looking everywhere but her as if he'd dismissed her question. Dax shifted his weight and gave Allie a questioning look. She shook her head. Now wasn't the time to get into it.

"I wanted to talk, just the two of us." He finally replied. "Can we do that, Allie? Just us?"

The way he said, "us" made a bitter taste rise in her mouth. They hadn't been an "us" in far too long, and even when they were, they weren't. Blake had simply wanted a girlfriend to look after him, fuss over him and be sexually available. He'd never been into her as wife material. It had been far too easy to use her, lead her along, rough her up a little, and then make her think it was her fault.

"It's been six months. There's nothing left to say."

Blake tugged his bottom lip between his teeth. His business suit was impeccably pressed, his brown hair stylish and combed to perfection. The lines of his tall, lithe form she'd once found sexy now held no appeal. How had she ever thought he'd be her husband?

Dax had made her feel more in the past twenty-four hours than Blake had in a year and half.

"I want a few minutes alone with you, please."

There it was, the demand wrapped up in politeness. He'd loved to use that tone on her when she wasn't doing what he asked or thought she should be doing. Like when he'd told her to sell the bakery, and she'd told him to fuck off.

"No." Dax's voice was concrete.

Blake simply smiled as he gave Dax a lazy once over.

"And you are?"

"An Alpha you don't want to piss off."

Blake laughed, but there was no humor in it. The sound made goosebumps raise over her arms. Inside, he was stewing and getting angrier by the second. She could tell by the way the vein on the side of his neck popped and the tension lines on his forehead. Allie could barely stand still. She was anxious and antsy to get Blake out of here so she could resume life as normal. The longer she was in his company, the more irritable she became. All he did was remind her of the pain, humiliation, and blatant self-hatred he'd inspired in her.

"I have nothing to say."

"Yes, you do!"

There was a shift in the air after Blake's outburst. Tension rolled off Dax with a kind of palpable vibration that Allie swore she could feel in the free space between them. His nostrils flared and his fingers flexed as if he were holding himself back from something. All she needed were these men to transform into bears and hash it out inside her store. She still hadn't recovered from the raccoon damage.

She'd placate Blake and get him the hell out of here before all hell broke loose.

"What do you want, Blake?"

She could barely breathe with both men getting tenser by the minute. She brushed past them both and went to the coffee bar. With trembling fingers, she began to fill the sugar packets. The back of her neck tingled as Blake shifted in her direction. Dax mimicked his movements, eyes riveted on his rival. Another low rumble shook the air, the intonation full of threat from Blake. From the corner of her eye, Allie saw Becks grab her cellphone off the counter and wrap it in her palm.

How had things gotten this tense?

Blake shot a hand through his brown hair. "I want my money, Allie."

She whipped him a look. "What are you talking about?"

Blake's hands sliced through the air, and he made a disbelieving face as if she were jerking him around. "Come on, I know you've heard that I'm getting married. I'm sure it burns you considering how often you begged me to buy you a ring."

At one time those words would have gutted her but now... she felt nothing but a mild ambivalence. It wasn't true; they'd rarely spoken about marriage, and she'd never once pressured him to get engaged. No matter what she said, he'd turn it around on her, so she didn't reply.

He shook his head and crammed his hands in his pockets. "I wanted to marry you, Allie. I did. But it was always one thing after another with this, this *place*. And then when I gave you the money for the convection ovens and you made no attempt to pay me back, I knew I couldn't marry a woman who would take advantage of me like that."

Her face went cold, her lips numb. She was so stunned; she couldn't respond right away.

"You didn't give me the money for anything. You... you gave me the ovens as a birthday gift."

She recalled how he had the delivery men wrap the twin ovens in a huge red ribbon and bows, and probably paid them extra to sing, 'happy birthday,' to her while they rolled them in. She'd drooled over those ovens since deciding to open Sticky Sweet, but the cost had been prohibitive. She'd mentioned it once to Blake and he'd surprised her with the purchase.

Never had they talked about the ovens being on loan instead of gifts.

He snorted a laugh. "Marybeth warned me the bakery was going under and you'd have an excuse not to pay."

Her brow furrowed. "Marybeth?" What did she have to do with this?

"Come on, Allie. No man gives a woman an eight-thousand-dollar birthday gift. I mean, Allie, honey, you were never worth that."

There was a crash as Dax pushed away from the table he'd been standing by and tipped it to the ground. In three big steps, he was nose-to-nose with Blake with an impassive expression that made him seem deadly.

"Outside." One word. Uttered with such force that Allie gripped the counter behind her.

Blake's nostrils flared as he glared unflinchingly at Dax. She shouldn't care if her lover gave her ex a taste of his own behavior. On a purely vindictive level, she wanted to see the inferior shifter get his ass beat. But she abhorred violence, especially if it was because of her.

"You were a horrible partner, Blake, and an even worse lover. I don't owe you anything."

His lips pulled into a thin line, the rise and fall of his chest matching Dax's.

"Insult me all you want while you write out the check, okay?"

"I'm not paying you back for something you gifted to me."

"You never had time for me," Blake hissed. He spun away from Dax to face her. Dax gripped Blake's shoulder, but it didn't deter him. "You were never worth my time. That stupid list you started? Oh yeah, I saw it. Add something else to it: Eats too many cupcakes. Seriously." He waved a hand suggestively at her body and frowned.

Dax grabbed huge handfuls of Blake's suit, and hauled him backwards so fast he tipped back onto his heels. Without mercy, he dragged the smaller man toward the door. Blake twisted, partially freeing himself. His hand shot around the back of Dax's neck and the two locked in a grip. In a blink, Dax gripped the front of the other man's neck with an unforgiving grip.

Blake's face turned red, then a purple.

"I'll shift and eat your fucking heart out. Do you hear me? You're nothing but a small, impotent bear. Completely unable to defend yourself against an Alpha like me. We're not done, do you hear me? But you are going to leave, right now."

The door slammed open with a resounding crack as Becks threw it open. Dax pushed his adversary through with an added shove that sent Blake flying. He pulled the door shut and flipped the deadbolt.

Allie slumped against the counter, her chest tight and breath coming in hard pulls. She wanted to shrink and hide, to just curl up into herself and turn off Blake's words. He'd seen the list. The one she'd felt compelled to write because he made her feel so small. There was no denying the truth anymore. Blake had always made her feel like less than he deserved, like an inferior woman because she had goals and aspirations that didn't include waiting and doting on him for hours a day.

It was shit. He was shit. She knew this.

But why did his words hurt so bad?

Dax took her upper arms in his hands, but she couldn't look up at him. It was embarrassing, humiliating that he'd heard what Blake had said. That list, that stupid list, was an expression of her dissatisfaction with her life and herself. It had never been meant for another's eyes—especially Blake's. The worst thing is that, though she'd used it as a tool to get rid of negativity, she'd instead, started to really believe there was something wrong with her. It had taken her so long to undo the damage Blake had done to her self-confidence and value of her own worth. And here she was, believing it all over again.

"Allie, look at me."

His soft, caring voice brought tears to her eyes. She couldn't do this right now. She needed time to process the humiliation and lick her wounds.

"I need you to go."

Allie stepped back; her arms suddenly cold where his hands had been.

"Let's talk about this."

She shook her head and studied the lines of her hardwood floor. "No. I don't want to talk about anything. Thank you for everything, but I need to be alone."

I need time to not feel worthless again.

Dax moved to her before she could react, taking her face between his hands and tipping her face up. His lips found hers in a kiss that poured out adoration like melted chocolate. It was quick, and then he stepped back and walked out the door before she could even catch her breath.

She stood where she was for several minutes. It seemed as if her rib cage had fallen out and left a gaping hole where a bright light of joy and confidence had just been.

It was a good thing she'd sent Dax away. If she hadn't been worthy of Blake, how would she ever make Dax happy?

She was too much to handle, but not nearly enough for a man like him.

Chapter Ten

♥

The asshole was easy to find, thanks to the stink of his cliché Old Spice cologne.

Anger brewed so deep and hot inside Dax; he couldn't let it go. He wasn't done letting the asshole know how he felt about his treatment of Allie. Dax never really appreciated how he could go into stealth mode, even while in his human form, until now. His footfalls made barely any sound and his body moved effortlessly through the blend of shadows and light. The sun was rising over the mountains, casting threads of orange and red all around as Blake reached to open his car door, seemingly unaware of Dax coming up behind him.

The bastard actually had the confidence to talk to Allie like that and think he'd walk away unscathed. He was seething inside, and his bear was burning to sink its claws into Blake's pompous face.

Dax grabbed Blake's suitcoat with one hand and pulled him backwards. The man grunted, his arms flailing as Dax spun him and slammed him against the car door. He took deep enjoyment at the fear on the smaller man's face. Dax put a hand to the base of the man's throat and squeezed.

"Some shifter you are." Dax smiled as a surge of predatory joy pumped through him.

Blake sputtered as he closed his hands over Dax's wrist and tried to pull him off. Flesh and tendon were slowly caving in beneath his hand as he applied more pressure. A purple hue took over Blake's face. Dax sighed. Smaller bears were so fragile.

Relaxing his grip, Dax leaned down close to Blake's face. "You're going to slink away and never bother Allie again, understand?"

Blake was clawing at Dax's wrists, his lips seeming to swell as his face changed colors.

Oops. Dax slid his hand to grab the asshole's shirt, glaring at him in demand for a response.

"Yes," he coughed out. "Okay."

"Whatever the fuck money you think she owes you is paid in full. If I find out you've been within a hundred miles of her again, you'll fucking owe *me*. Got it?"

He didn't wait for Blake's response. Releasing him with a shove, Dax strode away before his temper got the best of him. Sometimes the bear was hard to control and when his human side got pissed, it made it even more difficult. The animal stirred inside, making his skin itch and burn. More than anything, he wanted to go to Allie, gather her up and kiss her until she forgot all about Blake. But he was too agitated and close to losing his temper.

Something was majorly off with Blake's response to their confrontation. He'd been too complacent, too willing to let Dax dominate him. The man was a puss and he wondered what the hell Allie had ever seen in him? A shifter that would go belly up that easily wasn't worthy of any woman.

Dax cranked his neck to the side. When the need to shift took over, nothing would ease him until he let it out. He drove the curved road deep into the Rocky Mountains, stopping at the very tip of his father's land. Morning was in full swing by the time he got out and took a breath of heady, pine-filled air. Dax stripped off his shirt and kicked out of his pants. Naked, he stepped into a ray of sunlight and closed his eyes as warmth permeated every inch of his body.

With a cry, he threw his head back and let the shift consume him. His flesh gave way to a coat of thick, red-brown fur, his bones and tendons and muscles thickening into new architecture. Lobbing onto all fours, Dax gave a huge shake, the mass of his new body shifting side to side as sun warmed his coat.

Eagerly, he ran into the forest. With a roar, he tackled the base of a wind-damaged tree and wrestled it until it cracked. With his front paws, Dax pounced on the weakened trunk until it snapped with a resounding crack and fell. He turned to another for more of the same, and then another. Panting, he shook bark from his fur and realized he didn't feel any better. He was still edgy and irritable.

Allie.

He needed her. Now that he'd been deep inside her body, holding her against him while she writhed in pleasure, he needed more of her like he needed to breathe. He needed her in his bed every night, waking up to him each morning, sharing his home and his life. She'd obviously not been treated right by Blake. No wonder she was gun-shy about giving him a try, and her heart. Blake had dealt her a heavy hand in the confidence department.

He should have strangled the life out of that fucker.

Racing back to his truck, Dax burst up onto his hind legs and shook hard enough to shake the ground. His body popped and crunched as the massive animal sunk down into the body of a man. With a groan, Dax dropped onto his hands and knees and hung his head. The transition always stunned him for a moment as his brain and body caught up to the enormity of change. Struggling to catch his breath, Dax was about to flop over and lie on his back when his cell phone rang.

Remembering it was in his jeans' pocket, he rummaged around in the pile of clothes he'd dropped on the ground until he found it. Jett's number flashed on the screen.

"Yeah." Dax barked between breaths.

"Something's wrong with dad. Get your ass home. Now."

Dax didn't wait for his brother to say more. Slamming into his jeans and stuffing his feet into his boots, he jumped in the truck and took off, leaving his shirt lying in the grass. The road looped back down the mountainside, only a few miles from their father's.

He sighed in relief to see the healer's truck parked next to Jett's outside his father's house. Bursting inside, he was about to call for his brother when Jett stepped into the hallway.

"Calm your tits, Dax. He's going to be okay."

"What happened?"

Jett put a hand on Dax's shoulder and pegged him with a look. "You're not going to like this, but I swear... Dad asked if you were serious about taking a mate and I said — "

Dax opened his mouth to interrupt, but Jett slammed a palm over Dax's mouth.

"I said that you had a woman you were trying to win over. A good woman. One you were dead serious about."

Dax twisted his face out of his brother's grasp and slapped his hand away. He didn't care what they'd been talking about; he just wanted to know what was wrong with his dad. He hated to think his fears over his father's advancing age coming true.

"And?"

"He started to feel dizzy, like he had to sit down. Luckily, I was standing right beside him, so I caught him before he hit the floor."

"Well, what the fuck does the healer say caused it?"

A sly grin lifted Jett's lips. "Shock."

"What?"

"Dad was so surprised that you're actually thinking about meeting the deadline for a mate, he went into shock."

Dax narrowed his eyes and steeled his jaw. He sensed an air of jest in his brother's tone, but with Jett, it was hard to tell. He wasn't sure what to think. Yes, his father had been after him for a long time to do his duty and take a mate, raise a family. But...was it possible the still uncertain news could make him react like this?

A light chuckle came from the hallway. Trinity Ralston, the pack's healer, slipped his glasses into the front pocket of his button down as he came to join them. Patting Dax on the back, the elder healer shook his head.

"Not shock like what you're probably thinking. He's doing well, boys. What happened is perfectly normal, and given the news, expected."

It was Jett's turn to look confused.

Too impatient to wait this out any longer, Dax pushed past the two men and went to his father's room. He rushed in but paused when he saw his dad lying like death on top of the covers. His face was pale and relaxed as if in sleep. Lines dug from the corners of his eyes, as if he'd been clenching in pain. His hands, so huge and gnarly from years of shifting between human and bear, were eerily still. Even like this, Rowan was broad, hard, and imposing—too robust and rugged yet to be declining.

And this crap about being shocked over Dax's possible mate was a load of shit.

"Son." Rowan greeted without opening his eyes.

Dax gave a breath of relief. "I'm here, Dad." He went to the side of the bed, about to take his father's hand when Rowan began to slowly push himself into a sitting position. Dax hurried to help him. Rowan sat and waved his son off.

"I'll be fine."

Dax sensed his brother and Trinity as they stepped just inside the doorway.

"He's moon-downing." Trinity came to stand beside his patient.

He was familiar with the term but had never seen it happen. Not once had he even considered it happening to his father. Alpha males often started a stepping-down phase when their oldest son took a mate. It was a handing over of power, so to speak. Physically, Rowan would lose some of his intense strength and the natural drive of an Alpha to oversee, direct, and lead. He'd slowly weaken, losing his exceptional strength and heightened senses until he was basically human again. His ability to shift would remain, but the bear inside him would be a weaker, more placid version.

Rowan would essentially become less so his son could step into the lead Alpha role.

"But... I haven't taken a mate. Dad, I haven't mated her yet. You can't do this, not yet."

Rowan gave another dismissive wave of his hand. "I believe the pain of losing your mother kick-started this process years ago. The possibility of a serious mate for you turned the switch up. I can't help the hopefulness in my heart, Dax. My body took it as a sign."

Just days ago, his father had threatened to cut him out of the business if he didn't take a mate by the Pairing. He still had to convince Allie to be his. His father's biology was jumping the gun.

"There's one risk here," Trinity said pointedly at Dax. Jett came to stand beside them, his arms crossed and expression intent. Apparently, he didn't already know about this.

Rowan grabbed Dax's wrist.

"Unfortunately, my moon-downing decided to get worse right before the sacred Pairing. If you don't take a mate—if she won't have you or you decide she's not for you— the progression won't stop like it's supposed to. I'll continue to lose my strength and vitality."

Dax shook his head. "No. Dad, no."

"It won't stop until I'm dead."

Chapter Eleven

♥

"It's not a dead puppy on your plate, Allie. It's a piece of damn cake."

Becks nudged Allie with her elbow before sighing and sliding the plate in front of herself. With a grand wave of her fork, she eyed Allie before digging in.

Allie didn't give a shit about the white layer cake with lemon filling and cranberry glaze. She'd barely been able to give a shit about anything today. People hadn't stopped coming for coffee all morning, so she'd slid out a few plates of free cookies, too. She was grateful for being busy. When she had a free second, she sank into Blake's voice in her head reminding her of her faults.

Determined not to go down that rabbit hole, Allie got up from her stool and untied her apron. Becks gave her a questioning look.

"I'm going to check the cookie plates."

"They're full."

"Then I'll start on donut batter."

"Sit down and eat this with me."

Allie glanced down at herself, taking in the width of her hips and the soft rise of her belly beneath her sundress. "I'm good, thanks."

This was bullshit. She was comfortable in her body and this sudden self-loathing was a knee-jerk reaction to Blake being an asshole. She ran her hands lightly over her dress. Dax loved her curves. He'd dug his fingers into her hips and held her tight while he'd fucked her. Not once did he avoid kissing her belly or running his hands over the fullness of her thighs and ass.

So why did she feel so numb inside?

"I bet she's a total bitch." Becks licked the fork before diving in for another bite.

"Who?"

"Blake's fiancée. Think about it. That ass wipe cares more about himself than, say, orphans, or endangered whales or..."

"Dead puppies?" Allie finished with a small grin.

Becks waved her fork. "Exactly. What kind of woman marries a man who doesn't care about dogs?"

Her friend wasn't wrong. Blake had always been self-centered. But it had been easy to overlook because she'd loved him. Because she thought he was the kind of guy she was supposed to marry. And when he started saying unkind things to her, she overlooked that, too. When the unkind comments turned into outright derogatory insults and talking down to her, Allie tried to rationalize why he was doing it.

She tried to fix herself, so he'd be happier with her and stop.

She tried to change.

She tried to be better.

And she'd allowed the whole thing to continue because Blake was familiar, accomplished, and successful. He was prime mate material. Isn't that what every girl wanted? She'd thought so, until she woke up one day and realized what he was doing was verbal abuse. And then he'd snapped in anger and shoved her into a wall with a hand on her chest, preventing her from slipping away.

And now there was Dax, and he was... different.

With a wan smile, she grabbed the fork from Becks and took a bite of cake. Her hips were already cushy, so what was one bite of cake? She owned a bakery, for crying out loud.

"That'a girl."

Figuring she'd better see how things were going, Allie gave Becks a kiss on the cheek and headed out front. The bakery had quieted with only a couple of people milling around the coffee bar. Dax stood in front of the window,looking up with his hands on his hips. Her heart skipped a beat, as it always did when she saw him. He turned as if he sensed that she was there. For a moment, their eyes caught and all she could do was stare at his golden beauty. Was this gorgeous, strong man really interested in being hers?

He was everything that Blake wasn't. He was everything her soul and body and heart craved. How Dax had managed to get so deep inside her mind and emotions in such a short time confounded her. He could have any woman—Jesus, just look at him! — yet, he said he wanted her.

"Come look at this." He nodded for her to come over. She sidled up to him as he pulled a folded paper from his back pocket.

"Good news. What you've got up here isn't anything harmful. Some heavy-duty cleaner and fresh paint, and it'll be good as new. Here's a rundown of what I'm going to do for you."

His arm bumped into hers and he stayed there, resting his skin against hers. This was how it was supposed to be, she thought. Her, beside him, side by side. Dax handed her a paper. She tried to look it over, but she couldn't concentrate on anything but him and the emotions unfurling inside her. All the doubts were starting to fade. What if she really was his fated mate? What if she was supposed to have a lifetime with him?

He gave her a curious look. There was a handful of hope there, too. "What?"

"Nothing," she replied. She needed more time to figure out her thoughts before she dared to say anything to him.

"So, we're going to fix up the pipes in the ceiling that caused this mess, replace the part of the frame it damaged, and seal up around the entire building to stop the raccoons."

Right. She'd forgotten about the raccoons.

"I'm going to get rid of this little strip of harmless mold and give the affected areas a new coat of paint. I'll fix the walls and the woodwork. Most of my men will be involved in my family's gathering, so we'll start the day after and be done in less than two weeks."

The heavy, comforting weight of his arm slipping around her shoulders was unexpected, but she welcomed it by leaning her head on his shoulder. The strong lines of his neck begged her lips to cruise its length.

"Hey," he said while giving her a squeeze. "I'm going to make everything just as it should be, okay?"

"Even me?"

The words slipped out as they formed in her mind. Where had that thought come from?

"You don't need fixing, Allie. You're perfect the way you are."

He turned her to stand in front of him and took her arms in his hands. Her eyes began to burn as tears tried to push their way through. How many times had she longed for a man to understand her for exactly who she was? It seemed as if she'd waited a lifetime to have a partner who accepted her as is.

"I need to go slow, Dax. I need time to let this do whatever it's going to do."

Doubt flagged in her mind. Dax was the kind of man used to getting what he wanted, and he'd made it abundantly clear that he wanted her. Maybe he wouldn't want to wait.

Allie was about to throw her arms around his neck and lift herself up into his kiss when the bell over the door jingled. The man coming in had to duck to avoid smacking his head. Behind him, a not much shorter version followed suit. Dax jerked away from her, one hand sliding down her arm to grasp her hand and entwine their fingers together.

"Dad? Are you well enough to be out of bed?"

Dad?

Allie gaped at the older man, who was virtually a spitting image of Dax. The younger man next to him had raven-black hair, a bushy beard, and swarthy skin, so unlike Dax, though their features were eerily similar.

The older man stood beside Dax and crossed his arms. Her pulse raced at his intimidating stature. He was inches taller than Dax and bigger through the chest, with arms that could probably break a tree clear in half. Despite his obvious strength, lines of fatigue were etched around his eyes and a pale tint colored his face.

He raised graying eyebrows and pierced Allie with a stare.

"Is this her?"

Dax cleared his throat as if he were annoyed. "Here I thought you came in for sticky buns."

"I did. But this first. Is she?"

Dax turned to her. "Allie, my father Rowan."

A small muscle jumped in the side of Dax's cheek as he clenched his jaw. So, he'd told his father about her. She wasn't sure if she should be flattered or irritated that his family already thought... well, whatever they thought about their relationship.

"Yes."

"We have a problem."

Allie pulled away from Dax. She was curious what this was all about, but the sinking feeling inside said she might be better off not knowing. She tried to untangle her fingers from his, but he wouldn't let her go.

"What problem?"

Rowan's expression was equally hard and fatigued. Allie got the sense that when he was done with this conversation, he'd grab some sticky buns and take a nap.

"I got a call from Marybeth. Seems you had a misunderstanding with one of her fancy guests for her party— Blake something or other."

Allie put a hand below her ribs. That was the connection between them. She'd been confused when Blake had brought up MB, but now it seemed the two were cozy in some way. Blake never could let go of an insult to his pride. He held a grudge, a big one, until he felt he got even. Nothing had changed in the time they'd been apart.

Dax mimicked his father's authoritative stance. "I should have beat the life out of him for speaking to Allie the way he did. What's going on?"

"He said you choked him by his car."

"What?" Allie turned to Dax.

He made an unapologetic, so-what expression. "Way less than what he deserved."

The younger man pushed his way forward, hands in the front pockets of his jeans as he glanced around the store. Stopping in front of Allie, he offered her a rugged hand. She took it on rote.

"Jett Mitchell, Dax's brother. Nice to meet you. The problem is that Marybeth is so pissed over my brother's behavior, she's threatening to shut your bakery down if you continue to, as she put it, 'fraternize with that brute'."

Allie's face felt numb. "Shut me down? On what grounds?"

Jett shrugged. "Something about a rodent problem."

"Rodent problem? It was one raccoon!"

Allie put a hand to her forehead. Marybeth would not settle with a single raccoon but would use her shitty ability to fabricate a different story. One that likely involved an infestation of rats and rare but deadly Guatemalan cockroaches or something. And she'd spin it so expertly that the entire town of Estes Park would believe it... and she'd be ruined.

"Oh," Jett said nonchalantly. "She'll also pull her order and give it to Bella Blu if you don't comply. She wants your answer tonight."

Feeling as if the breath had been knocked out of her, Allie pulled up a stool from the coffee counter and plopped down on it. Dax was immediately at her side, his hand on her shoulder. There was little comfort in it. It wasn't that she needed Marybeth's massive order, or that she'd already purchased the bulk ingredients and gotten things started. With the order cancellation would come a pointed and poisonous slander of how Allie couldn't hold up her end of the deal. Of how Marybeth was slighted and forced to take her business elsewhere.

It was another form of ruin—delay, at the very least— that could do long term damage.

"Why the hell is this woman making you her messenger?"

Dax's fingers kneaded the tender flesh between her neck and shoulder a little too hard. Allie shrugged him off.

The elder shifter sighed. "I suppose she thought it would be more threatening coming from me directly. She's a pain in the ass, barely worth a second of my time. I'm only cooperating with her request because of the urgency you're facing Dax."

Dax's eyes went wide in that way people do when they want someone to secretly shut up. His father must have noticed because he closed his mouth and cleared his throat.

"In any event, I figured you'd want to know. Allie, it was nice to meet you."

The older man gave her a warm smile, but she couldn't return the sentiment. In the blink of an eye, things were threatening to crash down around her again. He wavered on his feet, causing both his sons to rush to steady him. Without a word, Jett and Dax assisted their father outside.

How dare Marybeth play at her emotions and her livelihood like this! Truth was, she did need Marybeth's order, so she could make her bank loan payment this month. With the moon party being the exclusive event that it was, hundreds of guests would get a taste of Sticky Sweet's deliciousness and it was too important of a marketing opportunity to pass up.

Staying away from Dax would keep Marybeth's mouth shut. But for how long? Sure, she could fill the order and run into Dax's arms after the party was over. But knowing the conniving woman at face value, Allie realized there would be a second wave consequence. Marybeth would find a way to make her suffer.

Worse, she seemed to have Blake in her back pocket.

Allie's stomach fell. She already knew how good Blake was at making her pay.

Chapter Twelve

♥

The bell above the front door jingled and even from the back room, the tingle that went down Allie's spine told her Dax had come in.

She didn't have time to fill Becks in on what Dax's father had said, and she was grateful. She had no desire to voice out loud that Marybeth was holding this over her.

"I'm cutting out early. You got this?" Allie gathered her purse and keys from the backroom and rushed back into the kitchen. Becks had her hands on her hips, her expression saying she was waiting for more information.

"Seriously, you're going to leave the woman who sleeps on a stool in the corner in charge?"

Allie grinned. "Smartass."

"Come on, tell me what's going on."

No. Because if she gave voice to it, she might change her mind. If she talked about it, she might not do the best thing. Impulsivity had always been front and center on the Loser Allie List. Instead of rushing into what her heart wanted, she was going to think this blackmail shit through and do the best thing, not the emotion-driven thing.

"I'll be back tonight. I've got to bake MB's shit."

"And the bacon cupcakes."

Ha. She'd forgotten about those. "The filling and frosting are made. Just bake and assemble."

And reserve one to rub all over Dax's body so she could take her sweet time licking him clean. He appeared in the kitchen as she was trying to pull her mind off that delicious scenario. The hard, sleek lines of his body only made it worse. Warmth pooled between her legs as sudden and intense arousal pumped through her. Just like that, her panties were soaked.

Dax gave her a questioning look and she didn't even care that he could probably sense the need in her. Of all the times for her hormones to go insane. It was probably stress from Marybeth's stunt. That, and the all-nighter she had ahead of her.

Or, maybe, it was because Dax was so damn hot, and it felt like forever since he'd touched her. Since his lips had cruised her neck, or his hands hand parted her legs so his tongue...

And Marybeth didn't want her to see him anymore? The woman clearly had no idea what kind of man-crack this bear shifter was.

"Come with me," she snapped, pointing at Dax before she spun on one heel and headed to the back door. She didn't need to look to see if he followed her. Every beat of her heart said that he was. Allie pushed out of the back door and made it halfway to her car before she stopped.

Turning to look at him, Allie was on the edge of a razor-sharp tension that her primal self said could only be smoothed one way.

Him.

Her nostrils flared as his scent wafted to her, her chest aching with her attempt to control her breathing. Dax observed her silently. His pupils dilated, taking up most of the amazing blue. His own breathing was coming faster, his body turning toward her as if he were trying to take up the space between them without reaching for her.

"I need you." The words fell from her lips, followed by a sob she couldn't control. Her lower lip trembled so she curled it inward and tossed back her hair. Damn it, she was in control of herself! She wasn't going to let that evil woman, or her psychotic ex, make her lose it.

Dax's lips parted, his gaze falling to her mouth. "*How* do you need me?"

His cocked his head, exposing the masculine line of his neck. The ache between her legs became a demanding, pleasure-pain throb. She resisted touching herself there, just to make it go away. Dax was so fucking sexy. She wanted to climb him, to jump on and ride until she collapsed in exhaustion—and then hop back up and do it again.

No way would one time be enough to kill this ache. This raw, powerful need.

With a little groan, Allie advanced on him. She grabbed the front of his shirt with one hand and his belt with the other, pushing him downward. With the raise of one eyebrow, Dax complied and sank to his knees before her. This was crazy. It was like some sex-crazed woman had possessed her body. She just needed him. Again, and again.

Threading her fingers into the hair at the side of his head, she pulled his head back and kissed him. Dax gripped her thighs right below her ass, his fingers like bands burning into her skin. Their tongues clashed and slid against each other as Allie leaned into him as far as she could. Like she wanted to melt into his kiss; to twine her body with his.

She pulled back enough to get a breath. God, he was so hot on his knees before her. So submissive and ready to serve. Dax's eyelids fell halfway as he gripped her hips and buried his face at the apex of her thighs.

Allie cried out, her hands gripping his head as he nuzzled the fabric that separated his amazing mouth from her skin. The tip of his tongue brushed against her sensitive slit. Even through the fabric of her red skirt, Allie felt the pleasure of his touch. Almost squirming with need, she adjusted her hips so his face fit against her thighs as his tongue swiped up and down, gently pushing and seeking until he made contact with her clit. Dax blew a hot stream of breath there, before closing his lips around her mound and gently sucking.

"I need more!"

He rocked back to look up at her. The sight of him on his knees like this was nearly her undoing.

"I know you do, angel. Do you have any idea what's happening right now?" A smile crossed his face like he was surprised and pleased and a little blown away.

"Yes, you're about to get fucked."

A deep sound rumbled from his throat. "Where? Where do you want to fuck?"

Her legs trembled, her pussy demanding more of his touch. Her place seemed hours from here. Going back in meant too many opportunities to be interrupted. She glanced at his truck parked on the far side of the back lot. It didn't matter where they made love.

She just needed it now, right damn now, before her body split in half.

"God, Allie. You have no idea what this is doing to me."

As if reading her mind, he stood and grabbed her hand, leading her to the truck where he threw open the back door. She slid inside, Dax pushing her down onto the seat as he crawled in with her and slammed the door. Bless tinted windows!

She clawed at his jeans, fumbling with the button and zipper, yet managing to get them open without trouble. Her body seemed to be on sex-driven autopilot... like something terrible was going to happen to her if she didn't get him inside her. Now!

"I need you," she panted. "I need you now, right now. Dax, please, please."

The words sounded jumbled to her own ears, but even as she pulled him closer and thrust herself at him, pressing against the erection he freed, he knew. The urges going through her were new and exciting and scary.

"Hold me down. Make me take it, Dax. Just... please."

His hand snaked to the front of her neck, his fingers closing over the base of her throat as he pulled off her pants with his other hand.

"Is this what you want? Is it?"

Her legs fell open as far as they could in the small space. Allie heard herself whimper as Dax slid the tip of his cock into her pussy and thrust deep. He applied more pressure, restricting her breathing as he began a hard, steady pace. She cried out over and over as pleasure came fast and immediate. She drew a deep breath around the pressure on her neck and the dual sensations of his dominance on her neck and his cock driving into her were almost too much to handle.

Suddenly, Dax withdrew and slid down her body, kissing a line from between her breasts and over her belly. He parted her pussy lips and gave a long, hard lick over her clit. Allie arched off the seat.

"You're so wet, you're soaking the seat, beautiful."

She could only moan in response and move her hips in a desperate attempt to urge him back inside of her. Instead, Dax laved her clit with his tongue, swirling around it and caressing back and forth. A tight spiral of sensation snapped, and an orgasm came over her fast, hard.

Blinding.

Allie grabbed his hair and screamed as pleasure dictated her body and clouded her mind.

Suddenly, he was inside her again, lifting her knees to grip his sides as his powerful hips slammed against her. She came again, with a gush this time that soaked the seat beneath her ass. Her mind was crazed, like she was losing touch with reality. All she needed was this powerful mating, this intense connection. Without it she would die. She'd be incomplete and unfulfilled.

Dax grabbed her hair and mercilessly pulled her head to the side. His teeth grazed her neck, sending little shockwaves over her body. Then a pinch, harder as he bit the tender flesh. His cock swelled, filling her to the hilt... rubbing that spot inside that made her come undone.

With a hard thrust, Dax bit intentionally hard on her flesh as he pulled out and came against her thigh. Crying out, Allie sat halfway and wrapped her arms around his neck, hanging on for dear life as her orgasm drew out.

"Oh God, oh God, oh God," she whispered, unable to let go. Never wanting to. Dax smoothed her hair and whispered things she couldn't comprehend. Her body went slack as a deep satiation soaked every inch of her body and soul. She'd never felt so relaxed... so free.

"Allie." Dax kissed her cheek and laid her back, doing his best to curl up with her on the seat. His skin was hot and slick with sweat. "Did you feel that? Do you feel it now?"

She could only nod, knowing what he was trying to say.

"You're my mate. You are. Don't deny me. I need you."

Their eyes locked and she lost herself more deeply in the sincerity of his blue depths.

"It's too fast..."

His cell phone rang, breaking the silence. He groaned and grappled to right his disheveled jeans.

"Yeah? Yeah, I'll be right there."

He ended the call and took her face between his hands to deliver a kiss so sweet, so decadent, it brought tears to her eyes. It was all he needed to say. How could she deny the connection between them anymore? Yes, it happened fast and with an intensity that completely pushed her off center. Maybe it was the indescribable sex they'd just had, but she didn't want to fight this anymore. Dax wanted her for who she was, flaws and complications and all. Fate had helped by throwing in a hefty dose of attraction between them. The more time she spent with him, the stronger the connection grew.

"God, Allie, yes. You have no idea how much I need you."

His phone rang again. Instead of answering, Dax kissed her forehead and smoothed a thumb over her cheek.

"I need to help my family for a few. I'll be back tonight."

"Okay."

Dax helped her straighten her clothes before she slid out of the truck. She walked back into the bakery, heart soaring. She couldn't recall the last time her heart had been this full and happy. Whistling quietly, she was just about to go behind the counter when someone called her name.

She spun to see Dax's brother Jett coming up behind her.

"I forgot to grab some of those sticky buns my dad loves. Got any?"

His no-nonsense tone was a stark contrast to his brother's teasing undertone.

"Yeah, we have a few. You're welcome to take them. I'll box them up for you."

"Appreciated."

She went behind the counter to the bakery case and pulled out a tray of buns. Sneaking him a few glances as she prepared his order, Allie realized how much he looked like his brother. Jett's raven hair and deeply tanned skin set off the unique near purple of his eyes. His brow was set in a serious line, one he didn't relax very often and the faint lines around his eyes whispered of hours spent in tension. He was physically striking and also... sad? Like he was carrying anguish deep inside that couldn't be contained.

Curious what his story was, Allie handed him the box. "All set. My treat."

He hesitated before taking the box. He gave a nod, and looked like he might turn to go, but caught her eyes and held them without mercy.

"Don't lead my brother on. There's no time for false hope."

Allie paused mid-air in reaching for a paper towel. "I'm not sure what you mean."

Jett looked behind him as if to ensure they were still alone in the store. He gripped the bakery box hard enough to imprint the cardboard.

"He needs to accept a mate by the end of the full moon in three days. If it's not going to be you, you need to tell him right now."

Dax hadn't said anything about a timeline, nor had he directly asked her to be his mate. He'd said she was... implying fate or some divine intervention.

"He hasn't specifically asked me to be his mate." It wasn't a lie, just a diversion around what Dax had implied.

Jett frowned. "Knowing my brother, he hasn't filled you in on all the details. He's just come on to you hard and fast, trying to hurry you into feeling something for him. But there are dire consequences to your decision. If you don't feel anything for him, let him go so he can take another mate."

Allie dropped the towel. Her mind was trying to catch up while pulling bits and pieces of her and Dax's time together. He hadn't expressed feelings for her per se yet made them clear in the way he touched her body and the words he said. Everything he'd done, in some way, was to show her he was interested. Invested, even. Why would he consider another mate?

"Are you telling me that if I don't agree to be Dax's mate, he's going to dump me to find a woman who will?"

"Yes." His decisive tone stung.

Allie cocked her head and swallowed down the lump that formed in her throat. "Let me get this straight. Dax needs to take a mate ASAP or something bad is going to happen?"

Jett nodded.

"Okay, so why did he wait so long? I mean, why now?"

There's no way a man like Dax would have any trouble finding a woman to mate with him.

"He's... had a hard time settling down. But the timeline is pressuring him now so he's— "

"Settling," she said as tears stung her eyes. Is that what was going on? Dax had come on to her strong and fast. And while he hadn't asked her to express love or any emotions, really, he did try and convince her that she was his fated mate. Did he really feel that way?

You have no idea how much I need you. The words that had filled her with so much promise and hope were nothing more than a bid to meet his end goal. Was it all a lie to meet a deadline?

"Thank you for telling me." Allie cleared her throat, ready to be done with this conversation. "I'll speak to Dax about it."

Jett tucked the bakery box in the crook of his left arm and headed for the door. Allie wasn't sure if she was more stunned by Jett's bluntness, or Dax's possible fraud. She'd never once felt like he was playing her to meet his own end, yet clearly her radar and ability to judge assholes appropriately were off thanks to her relationship with Blake. Was Dax pulling the same rose-colored wool over her eyes?

A single tear fell down her cheek. First Marybeth's threat to do harm to Sticky Sweet if she didn't stay away from Dax, and now this.

The Loser Allie List was supposed to be a sarcastic reflection of her life, yet the more things piled up, the more she realized there was more truth and less sarcasm to the whole damn thing. Was she so pathetic that she was going to fall for a man's games again?

The buzz of her phone pulled her from her reverie. Marybeth.

It's five o'clock, Allie Mae. What's your answer?

Chapter Thirteen

♥

"I'm putting an end to this right now."

Ben waved a spatula at Allie, his jaw set hard. She'd never seen her dad look so stern. Since she'd filled him in on Marybeth's ridiculous threat, he'd gone from a passive, easy-going retired schoolteacher to an alpha dad who was about to go ballistic for the first time in life.

"I should have put my foot down with that woman two years ago. This is partly my fault."

Allie blew a piece of hair from her eyes and grabbed another tray of cupcakes from the oven. She and Becks had been working on MB's cupcakes. There were so many that every available countertop space was covered with them. Next, they'd fill and frost them all by hand, box them up and pop them into the cooler.

Tomorrow, Allie would spend most of the day preparing Dax's order and then she'd be done with this madness.

"MB's raging psychosis is not your fault in any way, Dad."

Becks interjected with mock surprise. "She's also not a loyal customer. She looked pretty cozy sitting in front of the fireplace in Bella Blu's yesterday."

"Oh really? And just what were *you* doing in Bella Blu's yesterday?"

Becks licked frosting off her finger. "Getting a cup of coffee. Their dark roast is so much better than ours." She snagged a finished cupcake and set it by itself on the edge of the counter. "That's mine. No touchy."

Allie couldn't help but laugh. "Noted."

Becks looked up, her entire body going still. "What's... that noise?"

Allie and her father stopped what they were doing to listen. At first, all Allie heard was the soft rush of the fans above the ovens. Then a faint scratching sound came through.

"What is that?" She looked at her dad who held up his pink oven-mitted hands and shrugged. The sound became louder.

Becks moved around her workstation and put an ear to the wall. "It's coming from inside."

She tapped on the wall with her fist and the sound scattered in different directions. Something squeaked. Becks drew back and whipped Allie a look.

"You have mice."

Allie threw down the empty pan she was holding and rushed over to the wall. The sound came together again, going up... up... up. They looked to the ceiling. A gaping hole looked back at them from the still-missing tiles.

Three little heads peeked over the edge, beady eyes staring down at them.

Allie screamed. Becks almost plowed her over as she skittered away, doing the eeby-jeeby dance.

"Dad, I have mice!"

"I see that, honey. Remember that pet mouse you had in 5th grade? Walter? Or was it Roy..."

"Dad!"

First raccoons, now mice. All she could imagine were the creatures plopping down onto MB's cupcakes and ruining the entire batch.

"We've got to get these cupcakes boxed up. I'll finish them a box at a time, but they have to stay covered." Becks was already grabbing large white bakery boxes.

This was a prolonged nightmare. All the things consistently going wrong was more than any sane person could handle. She'd never been to the anecdotal breaking point, but she figured she was close right now if the urge to simultaneously throw up and scream were any indication.

What else could go wrong? It was a knee-jerk reaction to think it, but she'd be damned if she was going to jinx herself and say it out loud.

"Oh my God, he's suicidal!" Becks cried out as she jumped back.

The first mouse divebombed onto the workstation, landing on Beck's single cupcake and tipping it over. It fell on the floor in a pile of crumbs where it lay in a lifeless, furry blop. Becks jumped back, bumping into Allie before she hid behind her like a human shield.

The other mice must have decided death by cupcake wasn't as awesome as it sounded and turned away from the opening.

"Is it dead?" Ben pulled off his oven mitts and nudged the rodent with his foot.

"Step on it!" Becks wailed.

"No, *don't* step on it!" Allie nudged Becks in the ribs with her elbow.

Ben gave it a gentle push and the mouse hopped up with crazy fast mouse superpowers, skittered over Ben's shoe, and made a mad dash for Allie. She tried to move out of the way, but Becks had her in a death-grip and turned her to prevent the mouse from chewing her ever loving leg off.

"Becks!" Allie struggled to get free, but it was too late. The mouse ran over Allie's foot and dug its tiny claws into the leg of her jeans. It hauled itself halfway up her leg before she could react. Becks screamed and ran away. Ben tried to slap the mouse with a wooden spoon... missed and cracked hard against Allie's thigh.

She cried out and grabbed the spoon on reaction and whipped it across the room. Everything seemed to spin around her. Pressure in her head made her want to explode. Tipping point, tipping point, mother-loving tipping point!

"Enough!" Allie cried out. She grabbed the mouse as it raced wildly for the waist of her pants. Its soft, furry body struggled in her palm as she marched to the back door.

"Rabies! Rabies, Allie!" Becks hollered from somewhere inside.

Rabies was the least of her problems right now. She loosened her grip and gave the mouse a gentle toss...

Right into Dax.

The rodent bounced off his thigh, squeaked, and ran into the night.

"Um, thanks?" Dax gave a one-sided grin, but all Allie was seeing was red. The pressure in her head got worse and she was so tense, she was trembling. Beneath her anger, another frustration started to awaken. The one between her legs.

"Hey, what's wrong?" His playful demeanor turned serious.

Dax moved to take her hand, but Allie pulled away. She couldn't let him touch her or she'd tackle him to the ground and ride him right there. For the second time, the raw, deep need unfurled in her body with a demand that was impossible to ignore. There was so much inside her head right now, she didn't know where or how to start. But she knew what hurt and bothered her the most. She hadn't had time, really, to think anything through. Not Marybeth's stupid threat; not Jett's admissions. And certainly not her feelings for Dax aside from how much she hurt right now.

"When were you going to tell me that you're under a deadline to get hitched?"

He blinked. "Who told you that?"

She started to seethe. Of all the things he could have responded with, he was worried about who ratted him out?

"Why didn't you tell me?"

"I don't know. I suppose I didn't want to scare you off."

"So, you came onto me hard and heavy, making a big thing out of simple, sexual attraction, to try and get me to, what? Agree to be your mate so you can meet a deadline?"

His face fell just enough that he looked hurt by her words. A little voice in her head said she needed to cool her shit down, but she couldn't.

"You *are* my mate, Allie. You can't deny what you feel for me."

"Really? I'm pretty sure that's called lust, Dax. I wanted you to fuck me. You fucked me. It was amazing. That doesn't mean we're fated to be together."

"Why are you pushing me away?"

"Because this thing between us started on false pretenses."

And you're going to hurt me, just like Blake did. I've worked too hard on loving myself and being comfortable with who I am to let that happen again. Her mind kept going, though she couldn't bring herself to say the words.

He shook his head. "I'm sorry about that, Allie. I am. It was never my intention to deceive you. What I feel when I'm with you isn't what you think. It's not simple sex; it's true connection. And you... you feel it too. I know you do."

She crossed her arms. His confession melted her anger a little. "Really? How can you tell?"

"Because you're in heat for me. Your body recognizes me as your mate, Allie. It threw you into heat, just for me. The sex in my truck? What the hell do you think that was?"

Her nostrils flared. He was crazy. In heat? What was she, a fucking dog? Yet, as strong as the lust had come on... as intense as her need for him to fuck her had been...

"You feel it again right now. Your scent is full of your arousal."

She breathed hard and deep, very aware of how tight her chest was with each breath; how her nipples perked and begged to be touched.

"Why do you think I wouldn't come inside you? We hadn't discussed any of this and I... I didn't want to get you pregnant yet."

Yet? No! She wasn't going to go there.

"You have to take a mate tomorrow night?"

"Yes."

She steeled herself. "If it's not me, it will be someone else? Just like that, you'll pick another woman?"

He worked his jaw back and forth and shoved his hands in his pockets. She felt the separation between them like a physical slap.

"Yes. I have no choice."

She looked up to the sky and took a step back. It wasn't rational; she knew that. But damn it! Blake had wooed the shit out of her, rushed her, pushed her into a serious relationship only to turn into a horrible man when she'd acquiesced.

Dax put his palms up. "I know this is a lot to take in. I wish I had more time to chase you, date you, and let things unfold a little more naturally."

"I'm having a hard time feeling special when you said you'll basically take the first woman who comes along tomorrow night."

Dax burst forward and took her arms in his hands. "Damn it, Allie! Yes, I will take another woman. If that's what I have to do, I will."

Her body seemed to deflate as she searched his face. "Wow, I love you, too."

A burst of loud silence stood between them. Where was this bitterness coming from? Disgusted with herself, Allie pulled back as tears rolled down her cheeks. He tried to follow her, but she put out a hand.

He stopped, his brow furrowed, and tense lines appeared around his eyes.

"Don't, Dax. Someone can pick up your bakery order after ten tomorrow. Have a nice party, and good luck with the mate thing."

"Allie!"

She went inside and locked the back door, then leaned against it as she struggled with tears. Why was she being such a bitter bitch about this? Why couldn't she just open her arms and welcome Dax in?

When was she going to stop allowing herself to be such a damn loser?

Chapter Fourteen

♥

He'd really fucked things up.

Dax watched the line of cars coming up the mountain drive. There were already a few hundred bear shifters on the property, setting up tents and campers and sleeping places under the sky. The party had been going on since early morning when shifters started showing up. It was mostly a free-for-all; mingle and connect and relax until the Pairing started tonight.

Tonight.

Tonight, he'd have a mate, one way or another.

His gut clenched. He should have been upfront with Allie from the start. But he'd fallen for this connection between them so hard and fast that he hadn't thought it through. He was living in the moment and peeking into the future, something he'd never done with a woman before. He had no idea how to develop a real relationship, to cultivate it. Damn it, he was going to figure it out… if it wasn't too late.

He pulled his phone from his back pocket to see if Allie had responded to his text. Nothing. He'd tried contacting her all day yesterday to no avail. He wanted to go to her, to get her to listen, but things at home kept him here.

"Dad still can't get out bed." Jett came to stand beside him.

"I know."

When Jett had called, saying their father was too weak to be upright, Dax had left Allie after amazing truck-sex and raced home. They'd taken turns watching over Rowan while the other helped direct people into the woods and clearings for the Pairing. Other members of the Estes Park pack were on site to help, and Dax was grateful. This event was too big for he and Jett to handle on their own, especially with Rowan ill.

Dax ran a hand through his hair and turned to his brother.

"You told her, didn't you?"

"Yep."

"Damn it, Jett."

Jett shrugged. "Honesty is never a mistake. I figured you hadn't come clean with her."

Dax couldn't be mad with his outspoken brother. Jett had always been cut and dry. What you saw is what you got, and hell if the man minced words. He'd been looking out for Dax's best interest—at least that's what Dax told himself—with his need to take a mate. For their father's sake.

"What did she say when you asked her to be your mate?"

"I... never actually asked her."

Jett grabbed the sleeve of Dax's tee shirt and yanked him, so they were face-to-face. "*What* did you just say?"

Dax broke free. "I'm an idiot. I didn't do any of this right."

Jett made a half turn in frustration and squared in front of Dax. His purple eyes were understanding but... not. "Fix it, Dax. For dad's sake, if not your own. Just, fix it."

Dax watched his brother storm off. He ran a hand over his face, turning to watch the road again. He'd been so willing to let the instant and powerful connection between them drive this relationship, that he hadn't done enough himself to win Allie over. Just because he'd finally made up his mind to settle down with her, doesn't mean she'd come to the same instant decision.

She'd already been burned by a shifter, that piece of shit, and what had he done to reassure her fears? Nothing. Her ridiculous Loser Allie List. What had he done to reassure her that it was untrue?

Nothing.

Fuck his impulsivity! He'd always been this way; stubborn anytime he felt pushed, but once he made his mind up about something, he went a hundred miles an hour to make it happen.

Allie was more cautious. She balanced him that way. If he'd only listened to her instead of pushing so damn hard, maybe she'd be here with him right now. Hand in hand, waiting for the bonfires to be lit beneath the fullest moon of the year so they could mate for life. Instead, she probably felt like she was disposable and replaceable because he'd be forced to take another mate if Allie refused him.

It was unthinkable. How would he be able to take another woman and make love to her beneath the full moon, fill her with his cum, and profess his undying commitment?

Unfamiliar pressure started behind his temples. Clenching his fists, Dax swallowed hard as he realized his eyes were pricking with tears. He had to save his father, no matter what. But only with Allie. It had to be her.

The impulse to go to her pounded full and hard in his body. Scanning the still-full road, Dax knew he couldn't go now.

Soon.

# # #

Well, here goes massive what-the-fuckery.

Allie smoothed her red dress, appreciating how the deep-V wrap top hugged her full breasts and made her waist look small. The color contrasted prettily with her half-sleeve tattoo. She'd piled her curls on top of her head in a messy bun with wispy strands hanging down around her face. A pair of flat gold sandals and a gold anklet topped off the outfit. Not too bad considering no part of her wanted to dress up for, or go to, Marybeth's party.

How was she going to make it through the night when her heart hurt, and her soul felt so damn heavy? While she was serving sweets to MB's guests, Dax would be looking for someone new. He'd have his choice—blonde, brunette, short, tall. Hell, he might sample a few before he settled on one. Allie frowned so hard; her forehead hurt.

While she was enduring MB, Dax would be fucking someone else. He'd be lost to her, forever.

Allie turned away from the mirror and left the women's restroom. She fought tears as she returned to the kitchen where sixty boxes of baked goods waited to be delivered to Marybeth's. Dax's order was gone; someone had come to get them earlier while she was at home getting ready. She didn't ask Becks who picked them up. She didn't want to know.

If Dax had just been honest about his intentions from the start... if he'd given her the chance to open up to the feelings between them without all the pressure, maybe this would have turned out differently.

"Yeah, and maybe if you'd just taken a chance, you wouldn't be smearing your mascara."

Becks handed Allie a tissue with a sympathetic smile. Allie took it as a tear rolled down her cheek.

"Did I say that out loud?"

"No, honey. I know you well enough to correctly assume what's going on in your head right now."

Allie dabbed at her tears and gave a humorless laugh. "You're right. I should have been willing to give it a chance, to just go for it... but I can't. I can't be that vulnerable again."

Becks picked up a stack of boxes and carried them to the back where Allie's delivery van was waiting. Allie followed suit, and they worked in silence until the van was loaded. Finally, Becks took Allie by the shoulder and gave a squeeze.

"Remember when you took a chance on this old, run down building? In the three years' since, you've encountered an electrical fire, had a clandestine stash of ten-year-old buried cocaine drug-busted from your basement, been ravaged by raccoons and generally gone through a lot of shit. But would you take it back and skip all the joy it's brought you?"

"I'd like the bank loan to go away." Allie tried to smile.

Becks rolled her eyes. "You suck at diversion. Well, would you?"

How can you compare a relationship to a building? Allie threw her hands up and looked around. Dax might be strong like the bricks that made up these walls, but that's where the analogy ended. She'd taken too many risks in her life and none of them had panned out very well. She loved her business but taking the leap into entrepreneurship had cost her thousands, with more on the way. She'd jumped in with Blake and had gotten nothing but fear, shame, and a bruised heart.

"I'd better get going, Becks."

Allie turned away as her friend crossed her arms and sighed. She didn't let her mind wander as she drove through Estes Park to the gated drive outside of town where Marybeth lived. There was a man at the gate who took her name, verified she was on the list, and let her through.

Her father was already here, and Allie hoped he wasn't rocking in a corner somewhere. She'd tried talking him out of attending as MB's date, but he didn't want to ruffle her bitchy feathers any more than they already were.

She drove up the tree-lined, inclined driveway, hating herself for being wowed by the forested beauty of MB's property. Ahead, the trees opened to a manicured clearing of lawns and massive gardens, with a sprawling, two-story log home as the centerpiece. She was directed up the circular driveway and around back where four large, white tents were set up. People milled all over the grounds. It was like something from an uppity British television show. Everyone had champagne flutes in their hands. The men were dressed in three-piece suits with colorful, patterned ties, and the women all had fanciful hats adorned with feathers and gems.

Apparently, you had to dress like an idiot to attend this thing.

A waiter offered to help unload the bakery boxes and directed Allie to a table beneath the dessert tent. Together, they arranged cupcakes, sticky buns, and other goodies, leaving the extras in boxes beneath the covered table for easy refilling. She thanked the waiter, and then unsure what to do next, pulled up a little stool and sat.

"No, no, silly girl. Stand up."

Marybeth breezed over with a smile that didn't reach her eyes. She wore a bright blue dress with a billowing skirt and a train that floated across the ground behind her. Eyeing the desserts with clear delight, MB tapped her fingers together as if she were trying to choose what to sample first. "You're the hired help, dear. You stand until you're dismissed."

Allie tempered the anger that flared to life. She'd offered to serve guests as a courtesy, so she could schmooze potential customers, not as a hired waitress. MB picked up a cupcake and turned it side to side, studying it like something might jump out and bite her. Finally, she looked at Allie, dipped her finger in the frosting and made slow work of licking it off. She swirled her tongue around the tip of her finger and thrust it into her mouth a couple of times. Her eyes locked with Allie's as she made slow work of sucking her own finger, in and out. If she was trying to be indecent, it was working.

"Mmmmm, yes. I think I'll give this one to your father."

"Marybeth!" Allie burst off the stool. That was it; she'd reached her limit. No more! "Your behavior is completely out of line."

The older woman gave a blasé expression and dug her finger into the center of the cupcake. She withdrew it and made a face. "Oh, dear. I think I've found mouse shit in your cupcake. Oh, Allie. No one will ever buy from you again. Bye, bye, Sticky Sweet."

Allie's mouth dropped. The mice in the bakery had been caught before they could—

"Oh, my God," Allie breathed. "You released the mice in my bakery?"

Marybeth took a bite out of the cupcake and tossed it at Allie's feet.

"I believe I'm about to get terribly sick from your contaminated treats, Allie Mae. I'm suddenly not feeling very well. Who would, after eating mouse shit?"

She grinned like she'd just won an expensive prize. Allie came around the table, equally at a loss of what to say and raging to unleash on Marybeth. She'd never been a violent person, but she was past her limit now and the urge to beat the older woman's face in was as instinctive as breathing.

Guests began to filter into the tent, *oohing* and *aahhing* over the vast selection. Marybeth spun to the group, waving them toward the cupcakes.

"They're delish! Try them! You won't regret it." With a wink, she glided away, leaving Allie shaking.

What should she do now? The cupcakes weren't contaminated; she knew it. The mice hadn't had the chance to mess with the food. But Marybeth already had it planned. She'd probably announce later in the evening, after her guests had sampled Sticky Sweet's goods, that there'd been an 'unfortunate' problem with the cupcakes. She'd pretend to get sick, drop a few hints at mouse poop, and everyone who'd eaten one would get sick too— thanks to the subliminal messaging of course.

Bye, bye Sticky Sweet, was right. She'd be ruined.

Allie watched with disdain as people enjoyed her food. Why? Why would Marybeth do this to her?

"Allie."

Her heart sank at the familiar gravel of Blake's voice. She put a palm out to divert him as he approached and turned away.

"Not now, Blake."

"Yes, now."

God, he was so much like MB with his fake smile and self-confidence, as if he could do anything and get away with it. He offered her his arm, thrusting it at her with purpose that said he wouldn't be denied.

"I'd like to show you the grounds. I know how much you love gardens but never had time to make one of your own."

She recoiled from him, quickly glancing around to see if anyone was noticing them. "No thanks."

Blake grabbed her hand and placed it on his arm, closing his fingers over hers so she couldn't pull away. "I insist."

A couple looked at them and Allie was very aware they were being watched. Breathing through her nose, she clenched her jaw and allowed Blake to escort her out of the tent. She barely noticed the colorful flowers or curated, circular pattern. Blake's scent assaulted her, making her stomach churn. He made small talk about the garden, and his hurried pace suggested he wasn't a bit interested in a slow perusal. Her heart skipped in warning as he led her across the lawn toward the tree line. They passed other couples who were wandering around, and that gave her some comfort. Blake's hand tightened over hers, making her fingers hurt from the pressure.

"Ouch, Blake!"

She tried to pry him off, but he pulled her into the trees. Daylight was receding, leaving behind a dark lavender haze. Allie pulled back away from him, her shoulder popping with the stunted effort. In a flash, Blake spun her and pushed her back into a tree.

"Sweet, sweet Allie." His hand slid up her throat to grip her jaw in his palm. Leaning his other arm into her chest, Blake stepped into her so his body blanketed hers.

"Blake, no!"

She knew struggling and pleading would do nothing to redirect him. Blake needed his ego stroked; needed to be validated in some way. If she listened to him spout off and then petted his ego a little, he'd let her go. She remembered what Dax had said about Blake being less than a Beta bear. He was small and powerless on the bear shifter chain of prowess. It's why he'd never been in a hurry to take a wife—his genetics weren't desirable like those of an Alpha bear. Nature didn't care if he mated or not, but an Alpha bear like Dax? Nature put the pressure on, gave him the best selection of mates to choose from.

Dax. Who was probably picking through an impressive selection of women right now. Women who'd be more than willing to take his superior genetics into their wombs and make him beautiful babies.

Babies that should have been hers.

"You pathetic little bear." She spat before she could stop herself. "You're at the bottom of your pack's hierarchy, which is why your such an angry, mean little asshole."

Blake jerked a little as if she'd affected him.

"Don't even get me started on the sad size of your dick." God, what had come over her? Allie's body pumped with the force of her anger. It was almost as if she could feel resolve steeling inside her. Enough! Enough of all this shit.

Blake's hand snaked to her throat. He squeezed, forcing her airway closed. Allie grabbed his wrist with both hands, raking her nails over his skin. Blood wet the tips of her fingers as she scratched hard enough to rip his flesh. Pressure ballooned inside her head, her chest spasming with the need to draw breath.

"Bitch." Blake hissed.

A roar cut through the air and the ground trembled. Her eyes rolled to the side where a shadowy flash played in her peripheral. Dax ripped off his shirt, his jeans dropping to the ground as claws arched from his human fingertips, flashing in the light.

The world went fuzzy, blackness quickly closing in. She reached for Dax, her hand trembling, begging to reach him.

Right before she fell to the ground.

Chapter Fifteen

Allie's eyes opened, and it was all the reassurance Dax needed to know she was okay.

Baring his teeth, he cranked his neck to the side and let the shift claim him. With a powerful shake, his body popped and stretched from human to bear. Dropping onto all fours, he watched as Blake's body twisted from left to right, his bear slower to morph. Massive paws burst from his human hands, a midnight black coat covering the rolling body. Even in his shift, Blake was smaller and no doubt weaker.

How the man thought he was going to win this fight was beyond Dax.

Dax reared up, standing on his hind legs, and stretching to a full seven-foot height. All his senses were more alert. He sensed it all—the rapid pound of Blake's heart and the ripe scent of his fear and anger. Allie's sweet breath and the soft swish of her pulse that said she would be all right.

Blake rushed Dax with unexpected quickness. Their bodies came together with a quivering clash. Dax wrapped his front legs around Blake, twisted, and threw the smaller bear to the ground. He waited until Blake righted himself, rose on his hind legs again, and bared his teeth.

Blake glanced at Allie, spun, and advanced on her. Her eyes went wide as the bear barreled down on her. Allie skittered around the tree trunk and peered around it. Dax burst after him, his jaws clamping on Blake's hind leg. Blood burst into his mouth as he sunk his teeth deep and pulled. The smaller bear jerked to a halt with a roar.

Blake flopped to the ground and twisted, his front claws swiping at Dax's face. A burning line sliced over his cheek as the claws made contact, but Dax refused to let go. Grunting, he jerked his adversary backward by increments until he was safely away from Allie.

Dax let go and pounced over the smaller bear. With a grunt, Blake scrambled to his feet, knocking Dax back, and burst out of the trees. Look at the little fucker run. Primed for the chase, Dax enjoyed the pursuit. They sprinted across the grounds, through the spiral garden. People screamed and jumped back as the black bear crashed through the dessert tent. Allie's cupcakes and sweets scattered everywhere. Frosting flung in all directions, splattering clothes and shoes as guests scrambled to get out of the way.

Dax didn't care. Allie—*his* Allie—had been through enough because of this dickhead. When he'd witnessed Blake grab her throat, his rage knew no bounds. Murderous anger pumped through him now and it wouldn't be satiated until Blake's fur and flesh ripped beneath Dax's claws.

He got the chance as Blake plowed through another table and skidded headfirst into a large water fountain. Dax rolled the other bear and pinned his shoulders. The smaller bear's head fell under the torrential spray. He gurgled and fought, but Dax only dug his claws in, satisfied as streaks of crimson began to run down with the water. The basin turned dark pink as Dax drew more blood. He bared his teeth and opened his jaws wide.

"Stop!"

Marybeth hefted a shotgun off her hip and cocked the trigger. Dax froze for a second, then slowly pulled back his claws. People clamored around them to get away, some watching from a distance. Their collective heartbeats were loud in his ears. He pulled away from his opponent and dropped onto all fours.

Marybeth had no idea he could be on top of her in a flash, knocking that fucking gun from her hands before she could even blink. But for the safety of the guests, he played it tame.

"You... you beast!" She lifted the weight of the gun higher, with shaking hands. Her gaze slid to Blake. "Go turn human or something!"

Her attention turned back to Dax. "And you! You are going to be caged up like the goddamned heathen you are."

"For fuck's sake, Marybeth, that's enough."

Dax turned toward Ben Rowe as he parted the crowd and came after the gun with an outstretched hand.

"Go back where I put you, Benny."

"I said, enough." He grabbed the barrel of the gun and pulled it from her hands.

Marybeth gasped, her face going red. "You're embarrassing me, sweetheart." Her voice had gone small and sweet as if she were talking to a child. This woman was loonier than a methed-up clown. She reached for Ben and tipped her head up, as if waiting for a kiss.

Dax looked toward the trees where Allie was, moving to go to her now that the threat of buckshot in his ass was gone. She was there, coming toward him them. Dax's heart soared.

She faltered a bit as she got within a few feet, her eyes searching his form with a mixture of fear and awe. Dax turned to her and slowly nuzzled her palm. She let out a breath and dug her fingers into his fur.

Ben sighed right before his voice dropped. "Marybeth, I didn't want you two years ago when you were sending me nudies while your husband, the mayor, was dying from cancer in your bed. I didn't want you when you showed up at my house in nothing but a trench coat and a smile the same day you buried him. And I don't want you now."

Her mouth dropped, her eyes bugging out.

Dax had never been so thankful for super-sharp hearing in his life.

Ben produced his cell phone. "I've saved all the images and dates you sent them; in case you'd like to see them again."

She put a hand to her chest, apparently speechless. Another damn miracle.

"Well, then, I suppose the local press would love a raunchy story about the town gossip. Unless you'd like to explain why you're fucking with my daughter." Ben's voice was louder now, clearly including Allie into the conversation. MB looked between Ben and his daughter, then straightened her spine. She rolled her eyes and patted her hair, clearly unhappy at being cornered like this. When she didn't respond right away, Dax took a step forward and growled.

She squeaked and stepped back.

"Fine. I've made a large investment in Bella Blu and there's simply no room for two bakeries in Estes Park. Sticky Sweet is a lesser business, so it has to go."

Allie stepped forward. "The raccoons, the mice... all this to try and shut me down?"

"Allie, your cupcakes are delish, but face it, you were never competition."

"And Blake?" Ben asked.

"He's a lawyer, of course. He... drew up the paperwork and took an investment percentage for himself. Now, let's talk about how you're going to — "

Allie stepped into Marybeth's personal space, nearly close enough for them to chest-bump. Dax's chest filled with pride at the steely confidence on Allie's face.

"Now we're going to talk about how you're going to pay for the damages to my business, plus the baked goods you still haven't paid for, and compensation for premeditated slander and libel."

Ben turned to Allie. "If she refuses, I'll let the editor of Estes Elite have the pictures on my phone. I'm sure the society page would love it."

Dax watched the scene play out, his heart pumping with pride and affection. She was standing up for herself, way up for herself, and the look of pure determination was a joy to see. All her inner strength, it was there, shining for everyone to see.

As quietly as he could in his massive body, Dax retreated behind the broken tent as his body began to pull in on itself. His skin burned and itched as human flesh replaced hide, and muscle and bone shrunk. Moments later, he stood, panting, and realized he was naked. And there was a group of people behind him.

With a little wave to them, he pulled a tablecloth off a table and wrapped it around his waist.

The moon was climbing high, casting a brilliant silver glow through the sky. He walked around the tent grabbed Allie. Dax scooped her up into his arms and held her tight. Ignoring the crowd, ignoring everything, he picked her up and cradled her into his arms and carried her off into the night. She tucked her head into the crook of his shoulder and neck as he brought her into the woods and found a small clearing in the trees. Moonlight shone down on the space, creating a fairytale when he set her down.

"You're bleeding." She touched his cheek where Blake had swiped with his claws. Dax hadn't even noticed. He didn't care.

"Allie, I'm sorry that I screwed this up. I should have been honest with you as soon as I knew I had feelings for you."

Her breasts pushed against the fabric of her dress, the neckline dropping low and giving him an exquisite view of her excellent cleavage.

"I have feelings for you, too." Her soft hand caressed his cheek and Dax leaned into her touch. "It was killing me to think you were with other women right now."

"Damn it, Allie! There isn't anyone but you. There could never be."

He looked in her eyes and cupped the back of her head with his hand. "I've never been in love. Not until you."

Her chest hitched.

"I know you wanted to take it slow, Allie. I know you didn't want to be rushed. All I can do is promise you that we'll take it all slow, everything. If you'll say... if you'll agree to be mine. Be my mate and I promise, we'll do everything your way. I know it's a lot of pressure, but..."

"Yes!" She threw her arms around his neck. "Yes, yes, I will. I'll be your mate."

His heart soared. "You're sure?"

With a grin, she traced his lips with her finger before she laid back and reached for him. He pushed her thighs open and knelt between them, suddenly aware that he'd lost the tablecloth at some point. Allie pulled apart the wrap top of her dress, baring her beautiful breasts. Dax's mouth went dry as moonlight washed over her full, gorgeous form.

She was going to be his. Every day, every night.

In one movement, he pulled down her panties and tossed them aside. He lowered himself over her and took one pert nipple in his mouth. Allie's fingers threaded through his hair as she brought her knees up and tipped her hips.

"Please, make me yours."

Dax guided himself into her slick channel, sinking deep with one thrust. His body lay over hers, his cock buried deep so they were skin-on-skin, connected in every way. She cried out and arched into him as he began to move and whispered in her ear.

"You're my mate. Our mating starts tonight with the blessing of the full moon and ends only with death. Say it to me."

She moaned, breathing hard as he thrust over and over. Dax's body tensed, already primed to pump her full, claiming her under the eye of the moon. This mating would be quick, powerful, and it was threatening to overwhelm him.

"Say it," he begged.

Her pussy tightened around him. She was feeling it too, the climax that would come on hard and fast, connecting them forever.

"You're my mate," she panted. "Our mating begins tonight with the blessing of the full moon and ends only with death."

"God, yes."

Dax petted her hair and wrapped his other arm around her body to lift her closer to his heart. She cried out again and again, her face a mask of pure pleasure. He lost control suddenly and with a powerhouse of sensation. It rippled through him, an orgasm that originated from every single inch of his body and pooled out through his cock.

Allie cried out into the night. Her thighs squeezed him, her pelvis grinding into him as he came inside her for the first time, filling her completely.

Leaving no argument that she was his.

Gasping for breath, Dax rolled onto his back and pulled her on top of him. She smiled against his chest, then propped herself up on one elbow to look down at him. Moonlight swathed her like a halo, and he swore she was the most fucking beautiful woman he'd ever seen. He couldn't take his eyes off her. She'd never looked so content.

Allie grinned with her kiss-swollen lips and his cock flared to life again.

She toyed with his hair. "You know, staring costs extra."

Dax gathered her in his arms and rolled her onto her back.

"Name your price, woman. Whatever it is, you're worth it."

Rowan Mitchell didn't look very happy.

Dax was okay with that, because his dad was out of bed and as strong as ever, thanks to Allie. Even though she'd seriously displeased her new father-in-law by being out of sticky buns.

Sticky Sweet was packed, and the buns had been the first thing to sell out. Probably because she was serving them with a side of Jett's bourbon-infused honey and a new dark roast coffee that Becks declared was better than Bella Blu's.

The newly redecorated bakery looked amazing, thanks to Marybeth's blackmail money. With the cash, Allie had been able to refinance her loan and finish her dedicated kitchen for gluten-free goodies. *Ahhh,* the taste of revenge had never been sweeter, Dax thought, as he shoved another cookie in his mouth. He watched his mate working behind the counter, smiling and laughing, and fuck was she glowing.

"How many cubs is she carrying?"

Rowan downed his fourth cup of coffee and slid it to Dax to refill from the carafe.

"Two."

Dax ignored his dad's bid for more coffee because he couldn't take his eyes off his wife, or the belly that protruded proudly from beneath her blue checkered apron. He was a husband, and he was about to be a father. It couldn't be better.

Allie caught his eye and grinned. Pulling away from the counter, she grabbed something and came over to his table. Rowan's eyes lit up as she placed a plate with two sticky buns in front of him and gave him a kiss on the cheek. She pulled something from the pocket of her apron and handed it to Dax.

It was a little square napkin.

"Your idea turned out great," she said. "I'm still touched that you thought of it."

"I have a good idea now and then."

He laid the napkin out and read the words:

You have pretty eyes.

You're smart.

You're stronger than you think.

You're kind.

You make someone happy.

Oh, and you're hot. Don't forget that part.

Each line was imprinted in red ink, with a pretty, black border around the outside of the napkin. No more Loser Allie List, he'd told her. No more Loser Anyone List. He'd wanted to lift her up, and in the process, they decided to lift up every guest who came into the store.

The bell jingled above the door next to them, and a redhead walked in, eyeing the room as if she was searching for something. She looked a little lost, so he turned and handed her the napkin.

"Here you go."

She eyed him suspiciously. "Uh, thanks. Do you know where the bathroom is?"

He motioned the direction with his thumb, and she scurried away like he was infected with the plague. Allie sat on Dax's knee and laughed.

"You still have your touch with the ladies, I see."

He pulled her in for a kiss. "Doesn't matter. You're the only lady I care about."

"I love you, Dax," she whispered. And he held her close, his hand protectively covering her belly.

"I love you more."

If you enjoyed this story, please leave a review on Amazon. And don't miss the second book and third books in in the Estes Park Shifters series,

Keep reading for the first chapter of SWEETER THAN HONEY.

Connect

Connect with me at www.lizpaffel.com

Books by Liz Paffel

Available on Amazon and in Kindle Unlimited

Mates for Axxeon 9:

Axxeon King's Captive

Axxeon Commander's Pet

Axxeon Prince's Prize

Taken by the Axxeon

Cosmic S.W.A.T Series

Rescued by the Alien Enforcer

Alien Enforcer's Target

Detained by the Alien Enforcer

Alien Enforcer's Criminal Bride

Estes Park Shifters

Bear in a Bakery

Sweeter Than Honey

Bear in a Bookstore

Wild in the Woods

A Beary Wild Valentine's Day

Exclusive Bonus Story

Allie Mitchell.

His wife. His lifemate.

The mother-to-be of his cubs.

The woman who could terrify him with one narrowed expression of her pretty blue eyes. He was a grizzly shifter, for crying out loud. Next in line to become Alpha of the Estes Park Pack. He didn't back down from anything, run from anything, or fear any—

"How do you expect me to get *in* this thing?"

Well, maybe he feared one small human with a perfect baby belly, looking at him like he was the biggest of idiots.

Allie stood back with her hands on her hips, her upper lip curled as Dax proudly displayed the extra-wide, extra-deep clawfoot bathtub he'd just installed. It was a modern take on an old classic with the pretty lines of an original mixed with four body massaging jets and inset LED lights at the bottom that changed color and made the water glow. There was even a built-in diffuser for essential oils that sprayed a relaxing mist over the water. The claw feet and legs were made of black and white marble. He'd had them custom made because his mate loved the similar countertops in their kitchen.

The disgruntled expression on her face suggested maybe he'd screwed up. So much for her super early Valentine's Day gift.

"Uh, well, you put one leg over and in, and then the other."

Her lips pulled all the way to the side as she turned fully toward him and pointedly jutted her very pregnant belly at him.

"I can't tie my shoes, Dax. How the hell do you expect me to get in there?"

The tub was special order that he'd intended to have ready in February for the actual holiday, but the artisan had a much earlier opening and Dax grabbed it. Allie worked long hours at her business Sticky Sweet Bakery—too long most days considering she was carrying twin cubs—and she was completely drained by evening. She loved baths, so getting the tub sooner had been a no brainer.

He grinned, trying to diffuse her irritation.

"I could build you a ramp, like the ones people use so their old dogs to get on the bed."

He knew the moment the words passed his lips that he was in for it. Damn it. Moving in quick, he took her by the upper arms and rubbed gently. "I'm kidding, Allie. I'm kidding. You're *my* woman. I'm going to fill this tub and add the bath salts that you love. I'm going to light a few candles, get you some snacks. And then I'm going to strip you naked..."

Her eyes lit up.

"And I'm going to lift you in my arms, put you in the tub, and not bother you for an entire hour."

She hitched one brow. "Only an hour?"

Dax kissed her forehead, relieved that she'd relaxed some. Maybe he was off the hook. "I can't stand to be away from you longer than that."

"Oh, bull!" She laughed and playfully pushed at him. "It'll be supper time in an hour. How convenient, Dax."

He put his hands up, palms out. "I'm capable of feeding us. I'm ordering Chinese."

"We live on top of a mountain. No one delivers this far."

She had a point. Their mountain home was miles from Estes Park. But he had a backup plan.

"I've got it taken care of, don't worry."

"You bribed Jett with donuts from my bakery to stop by with the food, didn't you?"

Nothing got past her. His brother passed by their place on his way home anyway, so a little bribe was worth it to get him to drop off food on his way. Dax's stomach grumbled.

Taking her by the shoulders, Dax turned her and walked her into their bedroom. She sighed as she spotted the huge bed. His body lit up with a different kind of hunger. She wore a red bandana tied around her curly hair, a loose ponytail coming apart from the band. Working the knot of the bandana, Dax frees it, and it flutters to the floor. He removed the hair band next and slid his fingers into the hair at her temples. Allie moaned, her body going soft.

Slowly threading his fingers through her hair, he massaged her scalp and combed the strands until they fell loose around her shoulders.

"Ugh, you're so good at that."

Her neck loosened, her shoulders relaxed, as she lightly rolled her head in time with his movements. Working his hands down her neck, he massaged the stips of muscle between her neck and shoulders, then slid his palms down her sides to grip the hem of her oversized tee-shirt.

Tugging it up and off her body, he slid her leggings down next. Allie gripped his shoulders and stepped out of the pants. Her ripe, beautiful body set him completely on fire.

Focus, Dax!

Fill the tub. Get the snacks. Light the candles.

Stick to the plan, man.

He mentally detoured the words to his cock, but it definitely wasn't listening.

Allie licked her lips and glanced down. Slowly reaching a hand to his hip, she slid it down and gripped his erection over his jeans.

"You promised me a bath in that beautiful tub," she purred. "And you promised me food."

A groan squeezed from his throat. "I can't help it. You're hot."

"I'm the size of a shed."

"I know and I love it."

Taking her belly between his hands, Dax crouched and kissed her bellybutton. His cubs were growing in there and it took his breath away every time he thought about being a father. Not long ago, he nearly lost that ability because he'd waited too long to claim a mate. No woman had been the perfect match until Allie and her sweet bakery came along.

He knew the moment he saw her that she'd be his. It just took some convincing, and a few hundred cupcakes before she realized they were fated mates.

"You're ridiculous." Her attempt at chastising him fell flat as he gently pushed her onto the edge of the bed and looped his hands around her back to unsnap her bra. Allie quickly crossed an arm over her breasts.

"If you take this off me, I'll never get that bath. I'll do it."

She tipped her pretty face up with an amused grin. She's had a point.

"Fine. Stay here until I tell you when it's ready."

Allie moved up the mattress, sat back against the pillows and closed her eyes. She'd be asleep in no time if he didn't hurry.

Back in the bathroom, he opened the windows to let in the warm breeze. Leaves rustled from the oak trees outside and wafted a sweet and earthy scent into the room as he filled the tub. He dripped citrus oil into the diffuser, added Allie's favorite bath salts, and arranged the over-the-tub wooden tray he'd had made to fit the tub.

Then he set out the snacks he'd stashed earlier. Sugar free chocolate muffins with fudge frosting, raspberries, salty chips, and the seltzer water she drank by the vat. His chest expanded as he looked at his handiwork. Allie had done so much for him, and it made him happy to pamper her.

To his surprise, she was still awake when he fetched her from the bed. Grabbing her silky pink robe from the edge of the bed, he helped her sit up and slipped it around her shoulders. The loosened bra slipped down her arms and his breath hitched as he got a full look at her perfect breasts. She pulled the fabric together and wagged a finger at him.

"Dax," she warned. "Bath first."

"You make it really hard to control myself."

Dipping his head, he took her lips. She always tasted so damn sweet. Leaning into him, her breasts touched his chest. Her nipples pebbled beneath the thin fabric, pressing into him and jacking his desire. He lightly cupped her breast, but she slapped his hand away.

Pulling away with an agonized groan, he suddenly remembered that he'd left the box of chocolates he'd bought her in the kitchen downstairs.

"Go, get in the tub. I have to grab one thing."

She'd been so careful with her diet since finding out she was expecting, but she'd been craving caramel nut clusters from the chocolatier in town. He'd bought her a four pack so she wouldn't feel guilty about eating them all.

She smiled and sat up. "Okay, okay. I'm going."

Trotting down the double staircase, he was just about to the landing when he Allie shrieked his name.

"Dax! There's something in the bathtub!"

Racing up the stairs, he found her frozen by the bathroom door frame. She turned wide, unbelieving eyes on him and pointed quickly into the room. Water splashed from inside. Moving in front of his mate, Dax stepped into the room, homing in on the bathtub and the sprays of water flying over the side.

Alarmed, he stepped fully inside.

And a half-eaten cupcake launched across the room. The treat struck him in the shoulder, the frosting sticking for a moment before the cupcake broke free with a slurping sound and fell on the floor.

"What the hell?"

Just then, a little black head appeared over the side of the tub. An animal clambered onto the bathtub tray, its round body soaked and dripping. A raccoon! The tray wobbled, toppling treats into the water as the creature tried to get its footing. Setting all four feet onto the tray, it looked at Dax and locked beady little eyes on him.

"You've got to be kidding," Allie breathed from beside him. "What is it with us and raccoons?"

He'd first met Allie after a posse of drunk raccoons broke into her bakery and went ham on the place. He'd offered his carpentry services to repair the damages and the rest was history.

The animal picked up a bag of chips, staring them down as if expecting them to take it away. It slowly, methodically crossed the tray and jumped onto the far edge of the tub. The remaining contents of the tray scattered. The raccoon paused and reached behind itself to snag another bag of chips, then bolted to the windowsill and disappeared.

Dax worked his jaw to one side and surveyed the mess while trying to fully wrap his head around what had just happened. There was water and snacks all over the floor.

"There was a raccoon taking a bath in my tub."

"Yeah."

"There's no way I'm getting in there now."

Dax sighed. So much for an early Valentine's Day present. "I figured."

He picked his way to the window and closed it, then slipped an arm around Allie and urged her out of the room. He closed the door behind them. So much for her relaxing evening.

"You know, a massage would feel really nice."

She side-eyed him pointedly, then wagged her eyebrows. Dragging his teeth across his bottom lip, he scooped her up in his arms and took her to the bed.

"You don't have to ask twice."

He reached for the tie of her robe as she looped her arms around his neck. Dax lowered to kiss her, pulled the tie free...

Knock, knock, knock.

"Dax! I've got your damn food."

Jett's voice sounded from the entryway downstairs. His voice was muffled as if he had the door cracked.

Allie rolled her eyes and flung an arm over her forehead.

Dax groaned.

Knock, knock. "I'm coming in. You better not be naked. Where are my donuts?"

Allie sat up and pulled her robe together. "Alright, mister. This was your Valentine's Day trial run and it failed miserably."

He stood and offered her a hand, helping her from the bed.

"I get a do-over, right?"

Her eyes narrowed. "Oh, many, many do-overs until you get it right."

"We'll start with the massage after we eat."

She swatted him on the shoulder. "Nice try. You have a bathtub to scrub, sanitize, and possibly set on fire to make sure it's clean."

"How about after that?"

She tapped him on the nose before brushing past him and going to the staircase. "Oh, you'll be scrubbing for a very long time."

Dax rolled his eyes and smiled.

Fine. He'd scrub. Allie was his mate. And he'd do anything to make her happy.

On the real February 14th, he was going to make sure there wasn't a raccoon within five counties.